"FOR WHAT IS A MAN PROFITED IF HE SHALL GAIN THE WHOLE WORLD AND LOSE HIS OWN SOUL . . ."

When Collingwood replied, it was in a low, rushed tone, like a man rehearsing a speech. "Strike a bargain with him. Make the alien promise not to harm Tenon. Then go on television and tell Bernardi to give Tenon over. The Church has had to compromise all through its history in order to survive. It can compromise now."

"But, there is no guarantee of Tenon's safety," he replied gently. "Without a guarantee—"

"You make a judgment, in the absence of a guarantee," Collingwood broke in. "You judge that Zanla can be trusted, so you take the chance and save the world from misery and the Church from ruin."

"You are asking me to be a hypocrite, or a liar."

"I'm asking you to save the Church."

FORBIDDEN SANCTUARY

Richard Bowker

A Del Rey Book

BALLANTINE BOOKS • NEW YORK

To Mary Elizabeth

A Del Rey Book
Published by Ballantine Books

Copyright © 1982 by Richard Bowker

All rights reserved under International and Pan-American
Copyright Conventions. Published in the United States by
Ballantine Books, a division of Random House, Inc., New
York, and simultaneously in Canada by Random House of
Canada, Limited, Toronto, Canada.

Library of Congress Catalog Card Number: 81-68657

ISBN 0-345-29871-3

Manufactured in the United States of America

First Edition: April 1982

Cover art by Darrell K. Sweet

1

"I believe in One God, the Father, the Almighty, Maker of Heaven and Earth . . ."

Some days it was hard to pray. Angela's mind would float off in any direction but Heavenward. Today, for example, it started on music (what would be the Numian word for *counterpoint*? For that matter, what was it in Italian?); music was her job, today, and she wanted, as always, to do a good job. Then it drifted back (as it often did) to when she got the job: walking out of her class in Advanced Spanish and seeing the man dressed in the gray suit, incongruously formal for a California fall. "Ms. Summers?"

"Yes?"

"How long do you think it would take you to learn a language from scratch—just from hearing it spoken by someone who doesn't know any English?"

"Depends on the language."

"Would you like to give it a try?"

"Don't mind if I do."

"I believe in Jesus Christ. His Son our Lord . . ."

Well, her religion had caused them a minor problem or two, but she was too good; they had to have her. Her mind skipped to Bacquier, looking harried, a million decisions to be made, her little request one of the least of them. "All right, all right," he had said. "But you can't go alone. Security, you see. Can't have you people running around alone out there."

Security was all right by her—as long as her request was granted.

"I believe in the Holy Spirit, the Lord, the Giver of Life, who proceeds from the Father and Son. With the Father and Son He is worshiped and glorified . . ."

Now the end was in sight: something about the number of cycles that had been completed. And what had come of all of it? Enough to keep scholars busy for quite a while—until the ship returned. If it was going to return.

"They've got to come back," Colin had said. "We have too much to offer."

"That's right. Too much," Natasha had countered. "They're afraid of us."

Angela didn't like to speculate, but she did have one thought on the matter. "What if," she had asked, "they can't find their way back?"

There were still far more questions than answers. . . .

The priest plunged ahead. As usual, there had been no sermon. He had nothing to say, Angela supposed, especially to five old ladies and one stranger. That was all right: it was the ritual that mattered to her, even when it was trampled through by an overweight middle-aged man eager to get to his morning coffee and newspaper. *Ex opere operato*, she thought. She knew Latin too.

Numian was a bit like Latin, actually. Highly inflected, relatively few irregular verbs. She and her co-workers would write it all up, of course, and someday it might be declassified. It was odd, really, but more than one person had compared the Numoi to the Romans. There might be something to that; there might be something to a lot of things.

She left her pew to receive communion. The old ladies stared at her. She gave them something to talk about, anyway. She shouldn't be thinking of them, though, she should be praying. Why was it difficult to pray?

Her life was too full, too much had been happening the past few months. Her mind was too busy processing information. She was just a go-between, but so much of it stuck, and got in the way of what was more important. When it was all over . . .

But when she thought about it being over, she was sad. There would never be another job like this one.

"The Mass is ended. Go in peace, to love and serve the Lord."

"Thanks be to God."

The priest shuffled from the altar, and Angela slid

quickly out of the pew, feeling vaguely guilty over her dilemma. She genuflected and walked out into the cold and windy New England morning.

Her driver was waiting patiently at the curb, gloveless and hatless. Didn't he feel the cold? She hurried down the steps and into the jeep. The soldier barely nodded to her. As soon as her door was shut he sped off toward the compound.

She wished Paddy Maloney was still driving her. The ride was a lot of fun with him at the wheel. But shifts had changed or something, and now she had this tight-lipped Canadian who made sure she understood what an imposition this idiosyncrasy of hers was.

"Is this extra duty for you?" she asked as the white countryside slipped by.

He shook his head.

"Well, I'm sorry you have to stay outside in the cold. You *could* come in, you know. It's a little warmer inside."

He shrugged. "I'm used to the cold."

So much for apologies. They were nearly at the compound before he spoke again. "I used to go," he said.

"To church?" she asked hesitantly.

He nodded.

"Why did you stop?"

The high fence appeared in the distance. "I just stopped." He slowed the jeep.

"You could always start again," she felt obliged to say.

He shrugged once more. "Too late," he said. The guards waved them through.

The ship was a large, luminous blue pyramid, sparkling in the winter sun. One long, narrow staircase led down from just above the middle of one of the faces. At the bottom of it stood a couple of UN soldiers, staring stiffly forward. The first time Angela had walked up that staircase she felt as if she were taking part in some ritual—an Aztec maiden, perhaps, going to be sacrificed. But at the same time she had thought, inanely: they too use stairs. Can they be that different from us, if we both use stairs?

Now she stood near the bottom of the stairs, nibbling on a donut and hurriedly scanning an Italian dictionary of musical terms. She had missed breakfast, as usual, and there was no time for deep thoughts about the Numoi.

In a couple of minutes she noticed the group heading over from the motel, and she put away the book. She gave a half-wave to the other interpreters and nodded to Professor Contini. He greeted her effusively, obviously very excited. "Ms. Summers, good morning," he said in Italian. "This is a beautiful day, is it not? We will learn a great deal today."

The typical reaction. She had tried to warn him when they had met last night: this will be the most frustrating experience of your life. It will be like trying to learn about Mozart's music by reading a description written by a deaf person in a language you don't understand. And just when you think you're making progress, they will politely decline to answer a question, or your turn will be over, and the opportunity will be gone—perhaps forever.

Well, he would find out soon enough. "Is your tape recorder working?" she asked.

He patted his pocket. "Won't miss a thing."

"Then we're all set."

One by one they presented their ID cards to the guards, who checked a list and impassively nodded their approval. Then up the stairway, as if they were boarding a plane.

At the top, though, there wasn't a stewardess—or an Aztec priest. They stepped through an oval door, and were greeted by Samish.

"Hello, good morning," he said in wretchedly accented English. "I greet you in the name of the Numoi."

"Good morning," the interpreters mumbled in Numian, and Samish gratefully lapsed into his native tongue.

He read from a list not unlike the UN guards'. "Contini—music—with Master Zanla. Ryerson—zoology—with Associate Rothra. Chen—visual arts—with Associate Sudmeta. LaFlamme—mathematics—with Novice Lilorn. Please follow me."

They followed, down the corridor that was now as familiar to Angela as the corridor to her office at UCLA. But she knew what it was like for Contini, gazing at the intricate tilework, smelling the faintly unpleasant odor (too many of them cooped up here too long; yes, they sweat too), but most of all observing the yellow-tunicked creature in front of them. No, *creature* was wrong. Put Samish in shirt and slacks and have him walk along Main Street, and no one would take a second look. A little shorter and darker than most Caucasians, perhaps; bone structure a little off for an Indian. But still well within the range of human variability.

Only Samish wasn't human. Common ancestry (spooky thought), or similar evolutionary pressures? Angela didn't speculate, but it was certainly keeping a lot of scientists up late arguing. And the sight of Samish, she knew, was making Contini do a bit of revision on what the word *alien* meant to him.

When they reached the first room, midway down the corridor, Samish stopped, turned, and bowed. "That's us," Angela whispered. She bowed in return and led Contini into the room.

It was small and windowless. In the center was a black metal table; two chairs on the near side, one on the far side. Perfectly neat and symmetrical. Angela sat in one of the chairs on the near side. "This is Zanla's office," she remarked, motioning to Contini to sit down. "They call him the Master, which I guess is equivalent to a ship's captain."

"How do they choose who will speak with us?"

"Knowledge and interest, mainly. The four officers and Samish are the only ones allowed to converse with humans. I assume Zanla knows more about music than the other three."

"This Zanla—is he a good man, er, alien to talk with?"

"Well, he seems more interested in the information exchange than the others—probably because it was his idea—so I think he tries harder. But since he is the Master they often call him in to consult about something: whether they should answer a particular question, you know, or how much they should say. That can get frustrating." Angela decided to try once again. "And you know, Professor, he isn't an expert. He won't know a quarter of what you want to find out, and—"

"Yes, yes, we'll see."

He was too excited to hear such things. He tapped impatiently on the table and scanned his notes—enough questions for a month of meetings, Angela was certain. She took out her dictionary and studied it until she heard the door open behind them.

"I greet you in the name of the Numoi. Angela, good morning." Zanla bowed deeply to both of them and swept into the room. He was slightly taller than Samish, and slightly darker. He wore blue robes, and had a clear air of authority. Angela liked him.

She introduced Contini to Zanla quickly but formally. Zanla was scrupulous about learning names, and was quite good at remembering them—even if he couldn't learn an Earth language. Natasha thought their linguistic incompetence was all an elaborate pretense to gain them some kind of obscure advantage. Perhaps. But really, everything could be a pretense, if one wanted to be suspicious. Why believe we were the first intelligent race they had contacted? Why believe, even, that they came from outer space? Angela preferred simply to do her job.

Which began immediately, with Contini firing questions eagerly and hopefully, fretting every time Angela stumbled over a term or asked for something to be repeated. Theoretically, in the morning session the Numoi answered questions and in the afternoon session asked them, but as usual it wasn't long before both parties were stumbling over themselves to exchange information, each awed by the similarities and differences of their two worlds.

Luckily, in talking about music there was little need for the sudden awkward pause and the (apparently) sincere apology. "I'm sorry. I can't tell you that." Each side had things they had judged best kept secret, but their music was not one of them.

This problem did intrude on them, though, when Lilorn would knock on the door and bring Zanla outside for a whispered discussion. Mathematics, Angela thought. Always tricky. Natasha said there were more pauses than words during the mathematics sessions. Angela welcomed these respites, although they drove Contini into a frenzy of impatience. "Doesn't he realize—" Contini would begin, and Angela would give an I-told-you-so shrug. By the time the morning session was over he had gotten through a twentieth of his questions, and only reluctantly followed

Angela back along the corridor and down to the surface of the Earth.

"Not enough time," he said, shaking his head. "So much to learn."

"They'll be back," she responded, to cheer him up. "They've spent generations looking for another intelligent race. They won't just forget about us. They'll bring their finest musicians. You'll have jam sessions together."

Contini forced a laugh. "I have a lot to look forward to. Meanwhile, I must prepare for this afternoon. If you will excuse me . . ." He strode quickly off toward the motel. Angela followed at a slower pace, letting the cold air clear her thoughts.

She ate lunch with the other interpreters, and as usual the conversation revolved around words. Natasha, as usual, had a theory. "It will be the linguists who unlock the door to this mystery of faster-than-light travel."

"How's that?" Scott asked.

"Because the Numoi can hide everything else, but they can't hide their words—not if they want to communicate with us at all. For instance, have you noticed the way their number words correspond to their emotion words? *Eblo*— one, *ablo*—tranquility . . ."

"*Gava*—seven, *gavo*—uneasiness," Colin offered.

"But what does that suggest?" Angela asked.

"It's their approach to mathematics," Natasha replied.

"Sure," Colin said, "if we'd listened to Pythagoras we might be visiting the Numoi, instead of the other way round."

It was all too much for Angela. "Tell it to Aronson," she suggested. "Bright idea number 804."

"Well, all we need is for one of them to be true."

Angela finished her lunch quickly, excused herself, and went up to her small room on the third floor of what had been, until recently, a Holiday Inn. She sat by her window and looked out on the highway where now no traffic was allowed.

The aliens would soon be gone, she reflected, and this room would no longer be home. Back to running graduate seminars, grading dull papers, preparing dull lectures. Funny, they hadn't seemed dull before. One quickly got used to being at the center of things. A pleasant feeling, but transitory, like all the things of this world—and of all other worlds. She took her rosary beads out of her desk drawer and sat by the window, praying, until it was time for the afternoon session.

Contini worked her hard through the long afternoon, getting quite upset when she stumbled through a discussion of harmony and he sensed his chance slipping irrevocably away. Then Zanla was summoned again, and his mood blackened further. Zanla stuck his head in the door a moment later and said, "I hope you will not mind. There is a problem, you see, with the mathematics. I must help them."

"Of course," Angela replied. It was nothing to her.

Zanla turned around and motioned to a passing crew member. He muttered something hastily to him and turned back to Angela and Contini. "I hope you will not mind," he repeated, gesturing at the crew member, who stepped inside and stood at attention by the door.

"We understand perfectly," Angela said. Zanla bowed and walked quickly off with Lilorn.

"Damn nuisance," Contini grumbled. "And why do we have to be guarded?"

"If this were your ship, wouldn't you protect it from aliens?" This had only happened a few times before. The Numoi appeared to have rather rigid laws of hospitality that made them quite uncomfortable in this situation—but still, guests like these could not be left alone for a long period of time.

The Numoi's problem was an acute one. As one puzzled scientist put it, "These guys have conquered the Universe with a bow and arrow." Everyone had a difficult time crediting the notion that the Numoi's technology was at best early industrial. No computers, no telephones, no airplanes; it was doubtful whether they even had the internal-combustion engine. Many members of the Alien Study Team still refused to accept this, preferring to think that the Numoi possessed incredible cunning and acting skill than to deal with the alternative: that faster-than-light travel was somehow attainable by a preindustrial society.

And that was the Numoi's problem: the one thing they possessed that Earth could want, beyond the hazy benefits of cultural exchange, they could not afford to let slip away.

Angela wondered: if I had the run of the ship, would I be able to solve the mystery? Aronson and the other members of the team were forever pumping them for facts, details, impressions. "It's a puzzle," Aronson had said. "Anything you notice is worth reporting, because it might be a piece of the puzzle." What if there were strange devices in the base of the pyramid—could she describe them accurately? What if there were nothing at all? What if—

A movement at the edge of her field of vision broke her rambling train of thoughts. She turned her head. It was the guard, who had evidently moved gradually away from the door. So that he could see our faces, Angela thought. She smiled tentatively at him.

He bowed in return. "Do you speak the language?" he asked in a rushed whisper.

The language was Numian, and the answer was simple. But should she give it? The crew was forbidden to speak with them, she knew. The guard was clearly afraid—of her? or of the consequences if he was caught?

"I speak the language," she replied finally, "but are we allowed to talk?"

"Don't worry. The Master told me he would be at least twenty *vobi*."

The *vobi* was a short unit of time that Angela had forgotten how to convert. The response was not exactly what she had wanted. Her hesitancy must have been obvious, because the guard tried again almost immediately. "My name is Tenon," he said. "I would like to be your friend."

Well, she could not resist an offer of friendship. "My name is Angela," she replied politely. "I want very much to be your friend, too."

"Yes, yes," Tenon cried enthusiastically, causing Contini to look up from his notes.

"Are you supposed to be talking to that guard?" the professor asked Angela.

"It's all right," she said, although not very sure of herself.

He stared at her dubiously for a moment, then went back to his work.

"You are the first"—outlander? barbarian?—"I have spoken to," Tenon said in a lower tone. "I was afraid the Voyage would end before I had a chance."

"Your Master is—"

"Yes, yes. Tell me, Angela: is it permissible to ask questions of a friend?"

"Of course."

Tenon glanced nervously at the closed door. Angela didn't like this. "The Master has not told us of your *hasali*. Do you have the Numoi's *hasali*?"

The word was not easily translatable—belief system was what Angela and the other interpreters had settled on. Part of the problem was that Zanla forbade discussion of many aspects of the Numoi's *hasali*, so that the exact limits of the definition were vague. "I do not know the Numoi's *hasali*," she replied. "Humans have many different *hasali*. They do not all believe the same things."

Tenon seemed to reflect on this. "Tell me yours then, Angela," he said finally. "What is your *hasali*?"

Angela smiled. In less than twenty *vobi*? What did he want to hear about? Politics? Economics? Ethics? Just what *was* her *hasali*? She thought of morning Mass, the words of the Creed that had drifted across her consciousness. Not easy to explain *that*. But it was what he had asked for, and it was the truth. "I believe," she began, "in a Supreme Being Who created and rules the Universe. He chose to become one of us for a while, to teach us how to live good lives, so that we could exist with Him after we die. But humans would not accept His teaching. They did not understand Him, and they feared Him, and so—"

Angela fell silent. Why was Tenon acting this way? His face was animated, his hands were twitching, his whole body seemed to quiver. Was it excitement, or illness, or some totally alien response? "Is there something—?"

"And so they put Him to death," Tenon finally managed to whisper. "But He came back to life again, to show the truth of His message. Didn't He?" he asked, reaching out toward her. "Didn't He?"

"How—I mean, I don't understand—"

"Tell me," he said. "Tell me. Finish it."

"They put Him to death," she continued, barely able to think it through. "They nailed Him to a cross of wood along with common criminals. But yes, to show He was indeed the Supreme Being, He came back from the dead, and showed Himself to some of His followers. Not to everyone, though, because we must have faith in Him if we are to be united with Him after death. But how did you know? Surely Zanla doesn't—"

Tenon waved the explanation away. *"Vomurd,"* he said.

Angela was unfamiliar with the word. "What is that?"

"It is . . . it is when something unexpected happens which nevertheless is part of a pattern in things-as-they-are. I cannot—it is difficult to explain." He fell silent for a moment, swaying slightly in what Angela recognized as deep concentration. "What was His name?" he asked.

"Jesus."

That seemed to mean nothing to him. He thought some more. "If I tell you of this," he said finally, "I put my life in your hands. You will not tell the Master I have spoken with you?"

"I will tell Zanla nothing."

"And the other?"—motioning to Contini.

"He does not speak the language."

"Very well." He stopped swaying, but his hands still twitched with excitement. He began talking in a low tone, quickly, so that Angela had to strain to follow him.

"We Numoi rule over much of our planet, but there are other nations, other races. You perhaps know this. The Council could conquer them, I suppose, but it does not choose to. In a hilly region of the north there is a race who call themselves the Stani. There are not many of them but they are strong and proud, and they have never accepted the Numoi *hasali.* They have their own instead, which is difficult to put into the language. They say that there is . . . is *personality* in things-as-they-are, and that they— the Stani—will one day become the living focus of this personality. Is this clear at all?"

No, but there wasn't time to make it clearer. "Please go on."

"They have had these beliefs for many generations. But

over time their *hasali* has become coarsened—just like the Numoi's. Many of them began to believe that somehow it meant that one day they would defeat the Numoi and rule the planet themselves. So when Chitlan—"

"Who is Chitlan?"

"Oh, I'm going too fast. It's so hard. Chitlan was a Stani teacher. He was born poor and humble, but he became very great, and many people listened to him. He claimed— he said that he himself was not only the living focus, but the personality itself. He said the Stani had been chosen not to destroy the Numoi but to bring peace and love to the world, so that everyone could join in the unending happiness of sharing in the universal personality."

"My God," Angela whispered in English.

"This was his message to the Stani," Tenon continued. "He traveled throughout their land, performing wonders to show the truth of what he preached. Many believed him, but many chose not to, because his message was a difficult one. It was much easier just to hate the Numoi. So the rulers of the Stani plotted against him and they arrested him and—"

"They put him to death," Angela said.

"You see?" Tenon cried. "You see? And he too came back to life. Oh, they tried to claim it was a trick, a rumor spread by his followers, but that is nonsense. Too many people saw, too many people believe."

"And do you believe?"

Tenon moved his hand in a circle, gesturing assent. "Chitlan's followers have brought his message to Numos. They are persecuted savagely. But some of us believe. Some of us think the Numoi *hasali* is corrupt and dying, and that Chitlan is the future, Chitlan is the truth. Our belief has to be kept secret, though, or we too would be killed. Someday, perhaps . . ." He fell silent.

"What do you make of it?" Angela asked after a moment.

"They are the same," Tenon whispered slowly. "How could they not be? The words we use are different, but the meaning, the truth . . . they must be the same."

"We too were persecuted," Angela remarked.

"Did your Jesus live long ago?"

"Many, many generations ago."

"But His *hasali* survived?"

"Countless millions believe."

"Millions," Tenon repeated in wonder. "Perhaps there is hope for our future then." His hands started to twitch again in excitement. "One cannot ignore *vomurd*. The pattern is there. One must submit to the pattern. That much of the Numoi *hasali* is true."

"I don't understand."

"You humans have much that the Numoi lack, Angela. Zanla does not tell us crew members everything, but we know about your communications instruments, your calculating machines, your fast land vehicles. The Council will do much to get these things, because they will give meaning to the Voyages and power to the Numoi. If your leaders could only say: we will share our knowledge with you, but only if you let the followers of Chitlan be free to live by their *hasali*. The Numoi might agree. They might, do you see?"

He looked at Angela hopefully, yearningly. She shared his excitement, she wanted to help, but . . . he understood so little and asked so much. "I will do what I can," she said. "But I have no power. I don't know exactly what—"

The door opened. She stopped. They stared at one another, and she could see the plea in his alien eyes, and she realized she would probably never speak to him again.

"You are dismissed," Zanla said curtly to Tenon, who bowed and left immediately. Zanla sat down and inclined his head to Angela and Contini. "Please excuse the interruption. Now, we were discussing chord structures?"

Contini began in a torrent of Italian. Angela sighed, and struggled to do her job.

She sat by her window and stared at her notes. Writing them had been the easy part. The hard part was deciding what to do with them.

Tenon had not asked her to do anything, but her task was clear—and it was hopeless. To bring the matter before the proper authorities would be to have it quietly ignored. The UN would have no wish to jeopardize relations between the two planets for the sake of a tiny cult. Pressure would have to come from outside. But, as a member of the Alien Study Team, she was forbidden to say anything about the Numoi without first clearing it with Bacquier or Aronson. To do so without permission was illegal; it would certainly cost her this job, no matter how valuable she was, and possibly threaten her entire career.

Learning and teaching languages were the only things she could do well. The only things she enjoyed. Still, if she knew she could be successful, the loss of her career wouldn't matter. But how in the world could she do what Tenon wanted her to?

She looked out the window at the empty highway, and after a while she realized this was the wrong question. The question was: could she live with herself, could she face her God, if she did nothing?

She put on her coat and went outside. It took her a few minutes to find Paddy Maloney, talking with a couple of Canadians by the garage. "Could I see you for a moment, Paddy?" she asked as nonchalantly as she could manage.

Paddy smirked at the other soldiers. "Aw, she's forever following me around. It's disgusting." But he moved agreeably away from them with Angela. "What's up?" he asked. "Need to go to confession?"

"Not exactly, Paddy." She took a deep breath. "I have a friend in town. A very good friend. I'd like to be able to get off the compound for a couple of hours to see him tonight."

Paddy hooted. "A man, is it? Does the good father at Most Precious Blood know you'll be committing licentious acts of carnal depravity?"

Angela smiled in spite of herself. "I'll have to commit them alone if you don't get me into town."

"Oh, we wouldn't want that. Not at all." He pondered for a moment. "There's some fellows off duty going out tonight. We'll get something wrong with the jeep and take the van instead. Sneak you under the back seat. Show up at the garage around eight-thirty. What I won't do for a beautiful woman."

"How can I ever repay you, Paddy?"

He laughed. "Tell me the whole disgusting story tomorrow. That'll keep me warm on guard duty."

"You're a dear." She kissed him on the cheek and headed excitedly back to the motel.

Darkness was falling, and the alien ship glowed dully in the fading light. She gazed thoughtfully at it as she walked past. It—and everything—seemed different now.

2

Father Gardner came out of the church and checked to make sure the big oak doors were locked behind him. A couple walked by, heads bowed against the cold wind. Too bad they didn't see him, he thought. Good example, priest coming out of church at night. Even if it was only to check the furnace.

He strode quickly toward the rectory, crunching through the crisp snow. As usual, the sound seemed impossibly loud, and he thought: they are following me, matching their footsteps to mine. He wanted to look behind him. If he looked, they would not be there. If he didn't look, they would be there. That was how it was.

But if he looked (as he always did), and they weren't there (and they never were), then he would be a childish coward for giving in to such idiotic reasoning.

He looked. No one.

He sighed and went inside the rectory, double-locking the door behind him. He thrust the dirty parka onto the coatrack and made his way down the hall to the kitchen.

No good living alone, he thought as he made himself a cup of tea. That was the real problem: the big old house with just him in it. Not that he needed a wife, of course. What he needed was another priest. Someone to watch TV, have a beer with. Ed Finnegan, Charlie Connolly, Al Bernardi, any of them. All of them. The rectory had been built for four priests, but there hadn't been that many in it for half a century, probably, since the '50s, when they still had the school, the nuns, First Communion classes, May processions, the works. And now there was just him, saying a last-another-winter prayer over the furnace and going slightly crazy in the long, lonely evenings.

16

He snapped on the radio to exorcise his morbid thoughts. Not much luck. On the talk show they were discussing the aliens—there was no escaping them. The UN said they were leaving soon. Would they be coming back? Would any humans be going with them? Was the UN trying to hide something? No one had any answers, of course, but that didn't stop the questions.

And that was so very familiar: the old ladies clutching at him after Mass, calling him late at night, bursting into tears during confession. Are they going to destroy us, Father? Will they make us slaves, Father? Is this part of God's plan? What does this mean to our faith? They looked to him for guidance, and he had none to offer. Beneath the reassuring façade was bewilderment, and fear. And while his parishioners had mostly gotten used to the fact of aliens in their midst, his own fear continued, and grew. There was so much people expected of you, and only so much you could do. If only—

The sound of the doorbell shattered his meditation. "Idiot, it's not the aliens," he muttered to himself, but his hand was shaking as he lowered his teacup to the table. He shut off the radio and hurried back down the hall to the front door.

Was he presentable? Fly zipped, collar straight? You forget these things sometimes when you live alone. The doorbell rang again. He opened the door a crack, leaving the chain on.

It was a woman, knitted cap pulled down over her forehead, looking cold and worried. "I'm sorry to disturb you, Father, but do you have a few minutes you could spare?"

He slid the chain and opened the door, then stepped back to let the woman in. It was only when she removed the cap that he recognized her. It was the Woman from the Alien Study Team, the Woman with the Guard. What did she want with him?

"Are we alone, Father?"

"Yes, yes. No one around here at night much. Won't you come in, uh, Ms.—"

"Summers. Angela Summers."

"Ms. Summers." Her features were thin, dark, vaguely Mediterranean. Her black hair was pulled back severely from her face. She could have been anywhere from thirty to forty-five; she had that antiseptic ageless look of a professional scholar, or a nun. And she must be a scholar, of course, one of "them so-called experts" his housekeeper referred to. Beyond that—and the fact that she was obviously a devout Catholic—he knew nothing about her. "We can go into my office if you would like to, ah, talk."

"That would be fine."

His office was a mess, but the rest of the place was messier. It was a small room, cluttered with overdue bills and unread diocesan reports. On the mantel was a half-full bottle of sherry. Oh dear. Just a glass before dinner, but no one would believe him. "I'm sorry it's so chilly in here. Old heating system, you know."

"It's fine. Especially after walking up from the center of town."

"Oh, yes, certainly." What was she doing downtown? And where was her guard? "Please sit." He scooped yesterday's newspaper off a dusty wing-chair. She took off her coat and sat down, laying the coat on her lap.

She seemed quite nervous. That made two of them. She fiddled incessantly with her cap and avoided his gaze, obviously unable to begin. He sat down opposite her, and tried to help. "Well, Ms. Summers, what can I do for you?"

She looked up from her cap at him, and he knew she was judging him, trying to decide if this overweight, not very bright priest was the one to tell her problem to. As he squirmed under her gaze he suddenly found the right pigeonhole for her. Not a nun, but one of those fanatical laypeople who knew more about religion than he could ever hope to, the kind who come up to you after a decent homily and ask how you reconciled your position with Thessalonians 1:5 or something. And this, oddly enough, put him somewhat at ease, because, no matter how great their intellectual superiority, those people always had an implicit faith in priests. Direct channel to God and all that.

Finally she thrust her cap aside, leaned forward, and began. "The reason I'm so hesitant in starting, Father, is, well, I'm not supposed to be here. I'm on the Alien Study Team—you perhaps knew that—and we had to sign things when we joined, and I think I may be breaking a law by leaving the compound and telling you what I'm going to tell you. It's not easy for someone like me to break the law."

"Take your time," Father Gardner said uncomfortably. He had no desire to be involved in law-breaking himself.

"Well," she said. "I'm an interpreter—one of four people who speak the alien language. So I am involved with the aliens day in and day out. You know, I guess, how similar they are to us in many ways."

"I've read whatever the UN has put out, of course."

"Yes, well, there is another similarity. . . . Perhaps it would be easier if you just read." She fished in the handbag at her side and withdrew some carefully-folded sheets of paper. She handed them to him.

He moved the junk around on his desk and found his glasses. He put them on, acutely aware of the intense gaze directed at him. It made him feel as if he were taking a test, and as soon as he was finished reading the teacher would start asking unanswerable questions. But there was no escape. He read.

It only took him a few minutes to finish, but he continued to gaze at the last page for a while afterward, trying to sort out his thoughts. Then he silently offered the sheets back to her.

"Keep them," she said. "I'm afraid to bring them back with me."

Reluctantly he held onto them.

"What do you think?" she asked.

He wished Al Bernardi were here. Al would be able to handle this. He certainly couldn't. "Well," he replied slowly, "there is a religion on—on—"

"Numos."

"—on Numos which is sort of like early Christianity." He paused.

"Yes, of course," she said. "But what can we do about it?"

He looked at her blankly. First unanswerable question. "What do you mean?"

She reached for her cap and crumpled it impatiently. "I

mean: the followers of Chitlan are being persecuted. Their religion is in danger of being snuffed out. One of his followers asks for our help. Shouldn't we give it to them?"

"But how can we help?" he asked, exasperated. "And why should we? Just because this religion is *like* Christianity doesn't mean it *is* Christianity."

Angela abruptly tossed her coat and cap onto the floor and stood up. She turned to look out the window behind her at the mounds of snow and the dark outline of the church beyond. She's trying to control herself, he thought. She's reminding herself that I'm a priest and therefore worthy of respect.

She turned back to him finally but remained standing. "What you say is true," she said, straining to be calm. "But I think we have an obligation to find out more about it. On another planet, among another race of beings, a religion develops in a way that is startlingly similar to Christianity. Isn't it possible that this is more than a coincidence—that Christ brings His hope of salvation to every intelligent race in the Universe? Isn't it possible that the Numoi's finding our planet, and Tenon's finding *me* are more than just coincidences? Tenon called it *vomurd*, a coincidence that is part of a pattern. You see, I think that God is giving us an opportunity here, to save a new religion and revive an old one. Because if we discover that their faith is identical to ours, then it will help Christianity as much as it will help the followers of Chitlan."

Father Gardner looked at her helplessly. "You may be right. I have no idea. But I still don't know what you want from me."

She sat back down. "I think we—the Catholic Church—must do what Tenon asks of us. We must put pressure on the UN to make religious freedom on Numos a condition for further discussion with the aliens."

"But that's impossible. Even supposing Catholic pressure would have any effect, only the Pope could speak for the Church."

"That is why I have come to you," Angela said simply. "I want you to help me get in touch with the Pope."

Father Gardner leaned back in his chair and sighed. Laypeople never understood. They assumed if you were a priest you knew every other priest, and a few bishops and cardinals besides. This is Ed Gardner from Most Precious Blood in Greenough. Would you put me through to his Holiness? Thanks a lot. Couldn't she see he was just an anonymous priest in a decaying parish, unknown outside the diocese and only vaguely recalled within it? How in the world could she expect him to—

With a start he realized that that wasn't true, not exactly. He knew Al Bernardi. And Al had gone to school with—what was his name? Collingwood? The Pope's personal secretary, at any rate. Al had a couple of funny stories he told about that fellow. Yes, it was possible, he supposed, somehow or other.

And that made him more nervous than ever, because if he really could help her, then that meant he had to make a decision. He could hear Al's big booming laugh over the receiver: she says what? you want me to what? Damn it, why was this his problem? Why couldn't the aliens have landed in Japan, or Nicaragua, or Vatican City? Why did he have to decide?

"Look," Angela said, leaning close to him, "I don't know what you can do for me. Probably nothing. I came here because I didn't know what else I could do. I just knew I wouldn't be able to live with myself if I didn't do anything. The Church is dying, we both can see that. There are no more vocations, no more schools. People don't want a religion that's against all the trendy things: abortion, euthanasia, casual sex. What future do we have? The Pope himself certainly doesn't seem to know. But here we may possess the ultimate argument in our favor: the proof that our religion is true. Can we afford to just forget about it? Oh, I grant you these notes give us very little. But isn't that all the more reason we should try to study Chitlan's religion—to see how far the similarities go? And if they go far enough, maybe the world will finally be convinced."

Her intensity smothered him. Suddenly, in the chilly house, he was sweating. Perhaps the short chain of acquaintances that led him to the Pope was another in her pattern of coincidences. Perhaps he was a minor but necessary part in the working out of some immense cosmic plan.

Perhaps she was right: it might all be pointless, but how could you stand to do nothing?

He found himself praying, an activity that usually did not come very easily. And when he had finished he wondered why the decision had been so hard. "Let me make a call," he said, "and then we'll see."

"Al, this is Ed Gardner."

"Hey Ed, how's it going? Any of the aliens join your parish yet?"

"Listen, Al. I've got to talk to you about something pretty important. Could you come over right away?"

"Oh Ed, hey, I'd love to, but I'm *really* busy. And besides . . ."

"It's about these aliens, Al. I wouldn't ask you if it wasn't urgent."

"Jeez, you sound serious. Can't you spill it over the phone?"

"Not really, Al. Please."

"Well, okay. Give me a few minutes—I'll have to steal a car somewhere."

"Thanks. Thanks a lot, Al."

Father Bernardi strode in twenty minutes later, wearing a Russian hat and flopping overshoes. "Better be good, Ed," he warned as he flung his hat and overcoat onto the coatrack. "I had to pull rank on one of the scholastics to get the car. Good Lord, what if he leaves the order because of it? He's a quarter of the Jesuits' future in the New England Province."

"You be the judge, Al." Father Gardner took him to the office, where Angela sat sipping a cup of tea. "This is Angela Summers. She has a story to tell you."

Father Bernardi sprawled in a chair and listened, then read, then listened some more. "Fascinating," he murmured finally as the other two sat awaiting his verdict. "Probably a hundred different ways of explaining it, of course, if you're an anthropologist or something. All depends on the premises you start with. You want the Pope to push it from Catholic premises?"

"At least to publicize it," Angela replied. "Get it on the

news, get priests to preach about it, put pressure on the UN."

"That's a tall order," Bernardi mused. "Clement has his hands full as it is. This might just make things worse for him politically."

"That's his judgment to make," Angela pointed out. "If we don't tell him the facts, he can't make the judgment. Will you at least bring it to your friend's attention?"

"Oh, I wouldn't call Collingwood exactly a friend. He's not the kind of guy to have friends. Still, we are acquainted."

"Will you do it?"

He thought for a moment, then sighed. "Collingwood is nothing if not thorough. He'll need your statement signed. He'll also probably want the particulars of your background. To check up on you, see, find out if you can be trusted."

"Of course, of course," Angela replied excitedly. "When will you speak with him? The Numoi are leaving soon, you know."

He smiled. "I'm intrigued by—what do they call it— vomurd? Not very persuasive evidence, I suppose. If you're part of the pattern, though, it's . . . well, intriguing." He reached over onto the desk and grabbed the previous day's newspaper. He searched through a couple of pages, then began reading aloud. " 'POPE SENDS PERSONAL ENVOY TO BISHOPS' SYNOD. Monsignor Anthony Collingwood, Pope Clement's private secretary, arrives in New York today to attend the American Synod of Bishops at the Biltmore Hotel. It is expected that Collingwood will help map plans to fight proposed legislation to repeal the tax-exempt status for religious property. Also on the agenda will be a discussion of the theological implications of the aliens, and various proposals for changes in the liturgy. A Vatican spokesman said . . .' Well, who cares what the Vatican spokesman said. The point is, Collingwood's close enough for a visit, just when we want to see him. God works in mysterious ways, would you say?"

3

"They have a kind of sculpture," Sudmeta was saying. "Only it is not made with stone or clay, but with concentrated light, so powerful that it produces a three-dimensional image that one cannot tell apart from the real thing."

"Rubbish," Rothra growled. "Another lie to make us afraid. They go too far."

"But you've seen their communicators, you've seen their engines," Sudmeta exclaimed. "Do you have to see each wonder before you will believe in it?"

"Certainly. Why should I believe anything they say? They have every reason to lie, don't they?"

"Of course," Lilorn remarked, "if we were allowed off the Ship, we wouldn't have to take their word for everything."

The three of them looked over at the priestess Ergentil, who returned their stares impassively.

Zanla sighed. They were all tired and irritable. He had pushed them too hard, and these constant squabbles were the result. They were all angry with him, he was sure, but only Ergentil was in a position to say so. "What do they call this sculpture?" he asked calmly.

Sudmeta consulted his notes. "Holo—holo—"

"Never mind. Just make sure it's legible for the archive. Anything else?"

The officers were glumly silent.

"All right, now what happened on the lower level?"

"A fight," Rothra replied. "Clia was washing the floor, evidently, and Marshan walked over it while it was still wet. They are both in the infirmary."

"And these are the cream of the Numoi?" Zanla remarked.

"Perhaps we should leave now," Ergentil said, "before we start killing each other."

"The time for the Departure is set," Zanla responded coldly. "It will not be changed because of a floor-washing incident."

"I think there may be concern that this incident is a manifestation of deeper problems," Sudmeta said carefully. "Ships have stayed out to the maximum before, of course, but never under these stressful conditions. If there are a lot of bonding problems—"

"Then we will keep trying until the problems are solved. Are there any other topics?"

No one spoke.

"All right. Hand in your notes. Samish has the schedule for tomorrow. *Alm a Numos*."

The others muttered *Alm a Numos* and departed, leaving Zanla alone at the far end of the oval table. He took the notes and carefully filed them on the long shelves behind the table. The shelves were close to being full. When he was finished he sat back down and stared at the empty seats around the table.

He had little respect for his officers. They had expected an easy Voyage to a safe setting. How they had blanched when he had twirled them off in an unknown direction, guaranteeing them death or glory! Well, they had not died, but still they were querulous, fretful, immature. Clearly not fit material for the Council.

Clearly not fit. His hand tightened on the table as he thought of himself at the time of his first Voyage, a wide-eyed Novice eager to lay down his life for Numos . . . so he had thought. It is all so easy, until you are in the Ship, and you look into the eyes of your bondmate, and you at last understand what it is that they ask you to do. How could he judge these officers harshly? They grumbled, but they obeyed. What more was needed?

Ergentil, on the other hand . . . but it was not her place to obey. They were equals before the Council, though he was Master of the Ship. He didn't lack respect for her, he just couldn't deal with her. A part of him felt like apologizing every time he spoke with her, and he was strong enough now to despise such a feeling, and to dislike the person who evoked it in him. What he was doing was right, and neither his officers' complaints nor her cold stares would change that.

He tried to stop thinking, and listened to the silence in the room. He breathed in the alien air. "You will either be my greatest success or my greatest failure," his teacher Elial had said once. "Perhaps you will be both."

No, not both. Not both. He took the literature folder off the shelf, and began studying for the morning's session.

4

Al Bernardi swizzled his scotch and soda and glanced at his watch. He knew exactly how it would be. Collingwood would arrive fifteen minutes late, apologizing profusely but intimating that he had been delayed by matters of far greater import than a meeting with an old schoolmate.

And who could deny it? He had managed to put a reality beneath his surface, and if the surface still seemed unpleasantly affected, that might be because old impressions die hard. Or, more likely, because Collingwood was incapable of acting naturally in front of Bernardi; his achievements were meaningless when confronted with a person from his past. Like an adult transformed into a dutiful child before his mother, Bernardi thought. Our previous selves stay with us, ready to take over at the slightest provocation.

This provocation had been planned, of course. Bernardi had tried and failed to get Collingwood's room number. So he had checked the time the bishops' meeting would finish, and stationed himself in the busy lobby, like a spy looking for a man with a red carnation. He had sat there for over an hour as most of the American hierarchy trooped by. When he finally caught sight of Collingwood, it was almost too late to pretend a chance encounter. He would have preferred to have had Collingwood notice him first, but he was heading for the elevator deep in conversation with some cleric, so Bernardi had to cross in front of them, stop in feigned surprise, and say, "Hey Tony, this is my turf. You oughta have permission."

Collingwood looked up. The gears whirred and produced a smile and a handshake. "I have a papal dispensation, Al."

Not a bad response. No one could accuse Collingwood of

being stupid. "I'll let it go this time. But you'll have to let me buy you a drink."

The smile wavered. Was the hesitation real or surface? "Gee, Al. I'd love to, but—"

"Doesn't have to be right now. I'm going to be around."

A suitable pause to consider his schedule. "Ten o'clock in the lounge?"

"I'll be there."

And he was, wondering now why he hadn't been truthful with Collingwood. "I have something very important to discuss with you, Tony. Could I have a few moments of your time as soon as possible?" Why make a game out of it?

I'm no better than he is, Bernardi reflected. At least, the past affected them both in the same way. For if Collingwood were quick to assert his position, Bernardi could not help trying to deny its importance. To beg for a few minutes of Collingwood's time would be to admit his superiority and to accept a change in the roles Bernardi's memory had assigned to them. No longer could he be the wry, detached observer while Collingwood was the pitiful power-mad adolescent. That shouldn't be important, of course; the attitude was quite probably sinful. But it existed.

They had met as undergraduates at Fordham. He was the tough New York City kid, Collingwood the pampered child of a wealthy professional couple from upstate. They were drawn together by their religion, and by the growing feeling both had that perhaps they were prepared to devote their lives to it. That made them rare birds, even on a Catholic campus.

But two people with vocations can be as different as any other two people, and Bernardi quickly found he had little else in common with Collingwood. He lacked ambition, had a tendency to be lazy, drank a bit more than was good for him, refused to take anything very seriously. Collingwood, in contrast, was ascetic, deadly serious, and, most important, so consumed with ambition that Bernardi still had difficulty crediting it. Walking back together from Mass one morning, he had jokingly said to Collingwood that the only reason he wanted to become a priest instead of going into politics was because presidents only rule two hundred million people, whereas popes rule seven hundred million. Collingwood had laughed, but he had also blushed, and Bernardi knew he had cut very close.

But in those days Collingwood's ambition was forced to be rather unfocused. He was in love with power and its trappings, but what power was within range of a nineteen-year-old? He ran for student government but failed miserably; electoral politics wasn't his game. He got appointed to a faculty-student committee to restructure religious education, but its proposals were ignored. It was, oddly enough, a part-time job that gave him his first real taste of power. He became a typist in the president's office, and suddenly found himself with access to all kinds of information about what was going on in the school.

"It's great, Al," he had gushed. "I help his secretary with the correspondence. Did you know that Father Keenan was reprimanded last year for his relationship with a coed in one of his psych classes? That's probably why he's on sabbatical. And did you know that Father Heffernan has asked to be laicized? Wouldn't he be the last one you'd expect?"

Bernardi had felt obliged to shrug. "So what?"

"So what? Knowledge is power, Al. You've got to know what's going on."

"What're you going to do? Blackmail Keenan?"

"No, but I'll know enough not to ask him for a letter of recommendation. You've got to be on the inside to get ahead."

"So who wants to get ahead?"

The answer was obvious. Collingwood was not one to miss an opportunity. He got in good with the president, received recommendations from *him* instead of Father Keenan, ended up in Rome at Gregorian with all the rest of the future bishops and cardinals, then on to some post-grad study at Oxford, where he somehow managed to attach himself to Cardinal Herbert, whose coattails he held onto all the way to the top. Meteoric. And Bernardi had done things his own way, ending up out in the woods teaching obnoxious rich kids the rudiments of civilization.

And both of us are happy, I suppose, Bernardi thought. Odd how it turned out. . . .

"I'm sorry I'm late, Al. Somebody called me up at the last minute and I couldn't get rid of him."

"No problem, Tony." He should have known Collingwood would be subtler now, smoother. No need to say flat out how important he was. Let Bernardi guess who that "somebody" was.

Another difference: his accent had drifted into an odd Anglo-Italian mixture that would take some getting used to. The long, thin face was still the same, though, and the gold-rimmed glasses, and the small, suspicious eyes behind them. "You're looking good, Tony. What'll you have?"

"Oh, just a ginger ale. I have a long day tomorrow."

Bernardi ordered the ginger ale, and another scotch and soda for himself, and began to consider how to approach his subject.

"Still teaching up in Massachusetts?" Collingwood asked him.

Bernardi nodded. "Still trying to tame the little savages."

"You don't sound as if you're enjoying it."

"Oh no, it's fine, really. They actually seem to like me. I think I have some kind of knack for motivating them or whatever. It can have its rewards."

"I suppose so," Collingwood said with a shrug. "But I've always thought that you had too much talent for that sort of thing. It seemed to me that you were always too willing to take the easy way out."

Yes, he could have expected this too. The roles were reversed. Now Collingwood was being the detached observer, judging the quality of *his* life. "I wouldn't say that joining the Jesuits was taking the easy way out."

"Yes, of course. But you know what I mean. If you join the Jesuits, then teaching high school *is* the easy way out. Where are the books you should have been writing? The promotions you should have been getting? Don't you think you have too much ability to be where you are?"

The drinks arrived, giving Bernardi a chance to avoid an answer. The meeting had gotten off on the wrong foot. He should not be on the defensive, but Collingwood was obviously a much more confident and sophisticated person than the fellow he remembered. Should he just state his business then, and stop worrying about the dynamics of their ancient relationship?

Collingwood saved him the trouble of having to decide. "You must be fairly close to those aliens up there," he observed. "Have you seen them at all?"

"I've been past the outskirts of the compound, but no, they keep people—"

"Damn situation's quite a nuisance," Collingwood went on. "Clement just doesn't want to make any theological statements about it. That's partly why I'm here. This synod's supposed to issue a position on the aliens in the next day or two, and he wants to be kept informed. Collegiality's fine if you've got all eternity to make a decision, but this delay and vacillation really reflect badly on the Church, don't you think?"

Bernardi nodded vaguely, and jumped in. "These aliens, Tony—I have some information about them that I think the Pope should see." He took an envelope out of his pocket and slid it across the table to Collingwood. "Before you read this, let me tell you how I got hold of it."

He rather enjoyed the tale. Night-time summons, cold rectory, frightened woman: just the sort of thing to intrigue Collingwood, with his taste for secret plots. When Bernardi finished he was already opening the envelope and unfolding Angela Summers' notes.

Bernardi felt some trepidation as he watched him read. It would be easy enough for Collingwood to smile dismissively and end it all right there. That would not only prevent the truth about the Numoi from ever being known, it would also effectively humiliate Bernardi. He was supposed to have learned humility in the priesthood, but still he did not want Collingwood to do that to him.

After a few minutes Collingwood put the papers down and pushed his glasses back up his thin nose. "Not a lot to go on," he remarked dubiously, but Bernardi could detect the excitement in his voice.

"True," Bernardi agreed, "but what's there is pretty tantalizing."

Collingwood half-nodded and sipped his ginger ale. "There are alternative explanations, though. We don't know anything about their politics, for example, their intrigues on that alien ship," he observed. "What if this fellow Tenon heard about Christianity from some other human and made up this tale for his own purposes, to cause problems for the captain or the like?"

Bernardi shrugged. "I came up with a few what-ifs myself after I heard about this. Let's face it, you could what-if the thing to death if you wanted to. I don't think we should."

Collingwood said nothing for a while, conceding the point. "She wants us to speak out about this," he remarked, having reached another. "But it's certainly arguable whether that's in the Church's best interests. We talked about this taxation thing today. Now President Gibson has gone down the line with us on this issue. He's also risked his administration by giving the UN charge of dealing with the aliens. If we cause trouble for them over this when things have been running so smoothly, Gibson might just decide to switch his position. He could pull enough people with him to pass the bill."

"I understand," Bernardi said. "Of course I'm just a backwoods high school teacher—"

"Oh, cut the crap," Collingwood interrupted with a sudden smile.

"Well, at any rate, I don't know beans about international diplomacy or Curial policy. But it seems to me we're talking about entirely different orders of magnitude here. If there is the least possibility that the Christian pattern of salvation is being replicated on another planet, then by comparison it makes our American tax problems about as important as deciding how many angels fit on the head of a pin."

Collingwood inclined his head in agreement. "Just thinking it through," he murmured.

"Of course. I did the same thing myself."

"And you decided it was worth pushing?"

Bernardi grinned. "Worth pushing to a higher level. The higher you are, though, the tougher it gets. I don't have to worry about President Gibson."

"Yes, precisely." Collingwood shifted in his chair and

tapped the rim of his glass. "There's too little to go on," he said finally. "Even you backwoods priests know Clement. He'd want to call another Council to deal with something like this."

"But if you think—"

"What I think doesn't matter. My effectiveness depends on my ability to push the right issues at the right time. If I start annoying Clement then he'll stop paying attention to me."

"Good God, man!" Bernardi exploded. "Who gives a shit about your 'right issues'? It sounds like you've got a terminal case of tunnel vision. We're talking about the Universe here, about eternity, not Vatican chess games. You've always been obsessed with power, Tony. But power is useless unless you've got some perspective to go along with it. If this isn't worth risking something for, then I don't know what is."

Collingwood seemed shaken by his outburst. Probably because he still has enough sense to realize I'm right, Bernardi thought. His dilemma was clear, to an old acquaintance. This was a golden opportunity to score big, to solidify his position, to improve Clement's reputation and his own with it. But it was also a risk. If he failed—if Angela was lying or mistaken, if it was handled improperly, if there were unforeseen repercussions—then he failed big, and he would suffer the consequences.

Of course he might also be considering the good of the Church, Bernardi thought wryly. A man like Collingwood did not get where he was by being one-dimensional. But did he know how to separate his own good from his Church's?

Collingwood stared glumly into his glass, ran his hand over the envelope, sighed. "I need more," he murmured finally. "I can't do it for this. It's just a piece of paper. It could be a practical joke, a forgery, anything. Is there any way I can talk to this Angela Summers?"

Bernardi was taken aback by the question. "I don't see how, really. They won't let her out of the compound, because she deals so much with the aliens. Except for—" he smiled suddenly, seeing the answer, and with it the certainty of Collingwood's support. "Do you have access to a car?"

"I suppose so. What are you planning?"

"How would you like to attend Mass in Massachusetts tomorrow morning?"

5

Angela Summers genuflected, blessed herself, and hurriedly slid into the pew. The Canadian soldier had been late picking her up, and she had lost several precious minutes before Mass began. That was her best time for prayer: in church, alone with God, mind fresh and receptive.

She composed herself, lowered her head—and prayer came. Some days it was like that, as if God was waiting for you, ready to give your worn-out words new meaning, to lift the burden of everydayness from you. Perhaps it was because she had a special intention now, a reason to demand God's attention; perhaps it was because she had become a special part of His plan. No matter: the main thing was to pray, to feel God's presence.

It was not surprising, then, that she did not notice the man in the parka sit down next to her. He had to whisper twice to get her attention. "Someone wants to meet you," he murmured, smiling, when she looked up in surprise at him. He motioned to her to follow, and, after a moment's regret, she obeyed.

He went back to the rear of the church, then turned, past the unused collection baskets and the racks of devotional pamphlets, through a carved oak door, and down a dimly lit staircase. They came out in the church hall, with a small raised platform at one end and stacks of gray folding chairs along the sides. "I only come here for the AA meetings," he said, and led her to the back of the hall, into a small kitchen with a coffee urn and a refrigerator and more folding chairs.

In the corner was a sallow-faced man holding a small videotape recorder. "Good morning, Ms. Summers," he

35

said. "I'm sorry to take you away from Mass, but I'm sure you can understand how important this is."

"My driver is waiting for me outside," she said. "He will come in after me if I don't leave with everyone else."

"Father Gardner is going to say an extra-long Mass this morning," the sallow-faced man responded. "We will certainly be finished in time."

He motioned to her to sit down, and the two men quickly set up the videotape equipment. "I hope you don't mind," the first one said. "It makes a greater impact this way."

"I understand," she said. "I may be a little nervous, that's all."

And she was, at first, especially when she thought of who was going to see the tape. They asked about her background, and she stumbled through her degrees and fellowships. They asked about her job, and she forgot for a second the name of her university, then realized they were talking about the Alien Study Team.

It was only when they reached the meeting with Tenon that her nervousness fell away. As she described it, she began to recover some of the feeling she had just had in praying—the sensation that God was with her, that He was helping her do His work; and she found eloquence she hadn't thought she possessed in speaking about what had happened and how she interpreted it. She could say so much more in person than she could in her notes—about her sense of wonder as the similarities fell into place, for example, and about Tenon's last pleading look as their conversation ended. She had to make them understand: it was her mission.

And, quickly, it was over. The recorder was shut off, the sallow-faced man was shaking her hand and saying he would do his best, she was being led back upstairs, where the Mass had just ended and the old ladies were shuffling out.

"What will happen now?" she asked her companion.

He shrugged expressively. "God knows."

She hoped he was right.

6

It was when they began to watch it for the third time that Collingwood became sure that nothing would be done. Actually, he had suspected it ever since Clement had called in Fontanelli to view the tape with him. Clement's choice of advisers predetermined his policy. He knew what his Secretary of State would say, and that was what he wanted to hear. It was all so drearily predictable.

What Collingwood did not know was how conscious Clement was of this method. It was hard to credit a man in his position with such naïveté, but the longer Collingwood worked for him the more uncertain he was of just how much intelligence this Supreme Pontiff possessed.

He slumped a little lower in his chair; with the tip of his shoe he traced a pattern on the tastefully simple Oriental rug that covered the parquet floor in Clement's private office. He was travel-weary and in a sour mood. He had no one to blame but himself, of course; he had been carried away by rhetoric, by grand visions of interplanetary churches and turning points in human history. He had lost hold of his one great virtue: his clear-sighted pragmatism. And now he was committed to a position he knew was hopeless.

The tape flickered along. Clement sat bolt upright, hands folded on his lap, white skullcap slightly askew. He had seemed very interested at first, but now his face was expressionless, except for the tired air that had lately become a permanent feature. Next to him Fontanelli was tilted to one side, a cigarette stuck in the hand that supported his head; a legal pad lay unused on his lap. Behind his hooded eyes he could have been asleep. After a while he muttered something to Clement that Collingwood didn't catch. Clement nodded, and Fontanelli rose stiffly to turn the machine off.

Clement didn't speak until Fontanelli had sat back down. "Quite fascinating, Anthony," he said in his soft British accent. "I'm very glad you brought the tape to us. Now, what do you suggest we do?"

"Issue a statement," Collingwood replied promptly. "Carefully worded, not saying you necessarily believe that Chitlan is Christ, but that naturally we have an interest in studying the similarities between the two religions. Suggest to the UN the importance to the human race of seeing that the followers of Chitlan are not wiped out, and urge that they make that a strong consideration in their dealings with the Numoi."

"Couldn't these points be made privately?"

Collingwood shook his head. "Only by using the threat of a public statement. The UN has no reason to go along with us on this, and we have no power over it, except in the power we have to influence the citizens of its constituent governments. Ashanti would just put us off until the Numoi leave. Besides, the great value of the situation would lie in the public reaction to it. We have a chance to stir them up on our side, get them interested in religion again."

Clement glanced at Fontanelli, who was lighting another cigarette with his none-too-steady hand. "How do you feel about this, Carlo?"

The cardinal waved a cloud of smoke away from his face. "Let us assume the best case," he replied in his thickly accented English. "Let us say the girl is telling the truth—which I believe. Let us say this alien is telling the truth—which I do not know. Let us say things are as they allege—the religion exists, it is similar to Christianity, it is being persecuted. Still, I do not see how a statement like this can help matters. At best the UN is convinced to do as we ask; but I cannot see them convincing the aliens. If the Numoi are at all similar to the ancient Romans, as this girl suggests, then they both despise and fear this new religion. To allow it to exist would be unthinkable; it threatens their civilization. If the aliens offered America the secret of faster-than-light travel on condition that it become Communist, would America agree? In fact, I see exactly the opposite effect: the aliens become more determined than ever to stamp out the religion, now that they know it has support on our planet. I say nothing, of course, about the obvious political dangers we run by challenging the UN."

"You would do nothing, then?" Clement asked.

Fontanelli shrugged. "Talk to Ashanti. I agree he won't do anything, but at least he will be aware of the situation and understand our concern. Perhaps we can work toward something in future contacts, when the connection between the two planets is too strong to be broken."

Clement shifted his gaze to Collingwood. His turn. "What do you think of that, Anthony?"

He thought it was precisely what he had expected from Fontanelli: caution and shortsightedness, cleverly presented. He knew Clement would grab at the advice. It was the easy way out. Well, Collingwood thought, I won't give up without scoring a couple of points.

"This sounds like a conversation out of World War II," he remarked. "Our support will only harm the Jews, so it is best to say nothing." Fontanelli glared at him blackly, but Collingwood pressed on. "In any event, you ignore my main point. Private dealings leave the public unaffected. The world should know about this. It bears on the truth of what a third of its inhabitants profess to believe. Frankly, I am not particularly interested in launching an interplanetary crusade to save the followers of Chitlan. God will provide for them. We must tend our own flock. But to hide this from the flock would be a breach of our trust."

"I wonder," Fontanelli replied, "if this will have the marvelous effect you seem to think it will have. Even, once again, in the best case, those who want to believe will believe. Those who do not will find an explanation that fits their unbelief. The world will go on, as always." He stubbed out his cigarette and began to doodle on his legal pad.

Clement looked from one to another, slowly, his face a mask. You cannot bring this before the synods, Collingwood thought. This is your decision. This is why you were elected.

Clement stood up abruptly. "We will think about this

matter," he murmured. "We will let you know in the morning what we want done."

The other two men stood up as well. "I can have a draft of a statement ready for you by morning," Collingwood suggested.

Clement smiled. "Wait, Anthony, wait. You must be exhausted. Sleep tonight, think tomorrow." He turned to let his smile include Fontanelli, and walked slowly out of the room.

The two men stared after him. He was the one thing they had in common. "He'll never go along with this, you know," Fontanelli remarked conversationally.

"I know," Collingwood replied.

"Then why suggest it?"

Collingwood shrugged. "Perhaps one day he will realize he made a mistake, and remember who suggested the proper course."

"Then he will blame you for not being more persuasive," Fontanelli said with a dry laugh. The laugh turned into a cough, and with a half-wave he exited, his body shaking with spasms.

Collingwood waited until the sound of the coughing had died away, then he took the cassette and left the office, nodding absently to the guard at the door. He climbed the stairway to his own little room in the Papal Apartments, where his suitcase lay waiting to be unpacked. He slid it onto the floor and took its place on the bed. Glancing at his watch, he performed a quick mental calculation. Then he reached for his phone and dialed a number.

It took him about a minute to reach Bernardi. "He's thinking," Collingwood said. "But he won't buy it."

"What should we do then?"

"Nothing, at least for the moment. We have no options. Let me give you my private number here in case something breaks on your end."

"You feel bad about bringing it up?"

"It was my decision."

"Okay. Give me the number."

When Collingwood hung up he lay for a while in his clerical garb, staring at the ceiling. For some reason he began thinking about the day Clement had been elected:

standing in Saint Peter's Square and gossiping with some forgotten priest. They were waiting idly for the smoke to rise over the Sistine Chapel, not really believing that it would be white this time, not yet. But then there it was, gentle fair-weather clouds streaming from the ancient chimney. And what can compare with the excitement of the wait between the signal and the introduction, when the crowd suddenly swells to fill the square and it seems the Bernini columns will have to explode outward from its pressure? The two of them had made a final wager on who would be chosen (Collingwood had thought it would be a Third Worlder with acceptable Curial ties), and pressed forward toward the balcony. Finally old Pusateri had doddered out and croaked into the microphone the obligatory "*Habemus Papam.*" And then Collingwood had glimpsed Cardinal Herbert in the doorway. At first he was puzzled: why was he there, getting in the way of the new Pontiff? And then he stepped forward, clad in white, and the crowd roared, and Collingwood's companion was pounding him delightedly on the back, and the new Pope Clement raised his hand to bless the city and the world.

And then, Collingwood recalled, I thought to myself: I am smarter than this man. I am more intelligent than the Supreme Pontiff of the Roman Catholic Church. He had assumed that before, as a matter of course, about many different people who had stumbled onto great power, but never had its truth been as evident or as forceful as on that day.

The years since had done nothing to change his opinion. Neither had the meeting that had just ended. There was something intolerable about the situation that Collingwood just didn't know how to deal with.

The price of advancement was eternal tact, though, and he did his best. This man is a saint, he would remind himself, he has more charity and holiness in him than the entire College of Cardinals. And he did not do badly back in London, where, perhaps, holiness could still accomplish something.

But dammit, it wasn't enough to run the Church in times like these. A man was supposed to grow to fill the office when he became Pope. But Clement had seemed to shrink;

his virtues had become trivial, his shortcomings crippling. He was now timid, uncertain, afraid. And the worst of it was that he didn't seem to know or understand how ineffective he was.

No, the worst of it was that Collingwood had been with him every step of the way; Clement's failures were his failures. His mind wandered back even farther, back to his time at Oxford, to when he heard from a friend of a friend that Cardinal Herbert's secretary had cancer and was going to resign. "I'm going to get that job," he had said, and everyone just laughed.

"But you've never even met old Herbert," the friend of a friend said.

"Nevertheless, it's hard to ignore competence."

They remained dubious, and he set out to learn everything about the Catholic Church in England. After a month he talked his way into an interview, at which he swapped quotes from Newman, gave views that were a close fit to the Cardinal's own (although discreetly differing here and there to show he was his own man), casually mentioned his fantastic secretarial skills, and ultimately left Herbert no choice but to hire him.

Herbert was at the height of his reputation then, with the Race War behind him and the English church prosperous and influential. He was widely felt to be *papabile*, but Collingwood refused to consider the possibility of the Vatican. That would be asking too much: it would not come if he wished for it.

It had come, nevertheless, and with it the burden of the Pope's weakness. He had done what he could, but Fontanelli was right: in Collingwood's position nothing mattered if you couldn't be persuasive.

Collingwood took his glasses off and flopped over on his stomach. Not even Saint Paul could persuade Clement on something like this. It was asking too much: offend the UN, challenge the aliens, risk political revenge. When you cannot see the goal in the distance, it is best to take only small steps, because then you cannot go too far wrong in any direction.

And of course you end up going nowhere. Wearily Collingwood rose and dragged his suitcase back up onto the bed. It was time to unpack. Then he could obey the Pope's order and go to sleep.

Pope Clement was tired but did not feel like going to bed. It was a common situation for him, and tonight he did as always: he went into his private chapel to pray. Quite often Marcello would find him there an hour or two later, asleep, and he would fuss and fume about His Holiness's back and the necessity for proper rest. And he would be quite right. But was a little pain sufficient reason to give up praying?

He leaned back on the plush red velvet chair, his eyes fixed on the softly lit tabernacle. The room was as silent as—as outer space, although he knew a Swiss Guard was stationed discreetly somewhere nearby, and dozens of people were living out their lives in the Apostolic Palace, and millions doing the same in the city surrounding the Leonine Walls. Who among them had a better setting for prayer than he did? But then, who had more need of it?

Did the aliens pray? The followers of—what was his name? Chitlan? Of course they did. Did they dream that someday their leader would live in a splendid palace in the capital city of their persecutors?

Or no, carry it further: did they dream that their persecutors would one day be an ancient memory, and different people with strange new theories would be ruling in their place; that their religion would reach a peak and then somehow lose its grip on people's minds and hearts, and their leader would sit alone in his palace, helpless to stop what seemed so inevitable?

It was odd, Clement thought, but he had no difficulty in accepting the truth of what that interpreter had said. Of course the religion existed. Of course it was the same as Christianity. God would not leave any intelligent race without knowledge of His existence, without access to His grace.

But still that did not solve his problem. Collingwood and Fontanelli always seemed so secure in their positions. Even if they later reversed them (which sometimes happened), they simply adopted their new stands with the same certainty and forcefulness, never wavering in the belief that they had right on their side. How long had it been since he had felt that way?

He had read an article once that claimed he hadn't been the same man since the Race War in England. He had used up whatever reserves of courage and decisiveness he possessed in walking down that street past the machine guns trained on him and the barricades manned by hate-filled, frustrated blacks, death and fear almost tangible presences beside him. Some men can only do that once, the author had said; you can give them the Nobel Peace Prize afterward, and even elect them Pope, but you can't make them regain what they have lost.

Clement didn't know. Was it then? Or later that day, as he struggled to get through to Kuntasha, knowing that if he didn't all his courage would be wasted? Or, perhaps, was it as the ballots were counted in the Conclave, mounting inexorably toward two-thirds plus one, and he realized that a greater burden was about to fall on his shoulders than anyone should have to bear?

He didn't know. Something had happened, something had changed somewhere. He was not who he was, and tonight the thought of battling the United Nations and President Gibson and the Numoi filled him with terror. He had listened to all the arguments on both sides, and they had all made sense. There were always good arguments for caution, of course. So it came down to something other than reason, and the nonreasoning part of himself said he could not act.

They would write more articles about him, and gossip about him in the corridors of the Curia. Fine people like that earnest young interpreter would be puzzled and disappointed. But they were not Pope, and only a Pope can really understand. And life would go on, because not even the aliens could change a person's inner self.

A shadow fell across him. Marcello was standing in the doorway. "It is past midnight, Holiness."

Clement got up from his chair, genuflected, and blessed himself. "Another day," he murmured to Marcello as he followed him out of the chapel.

"And we are still alive, thank God."

"You are a pious man, Marcello."

Marcello shrugged. "It is not being pious to simply speak the truth."

They entered Clement's small bedchamber, and in the silent palace the Pope prepared to sleep.

7

Tenon had just been on guard duty by the officers' quarters on the first level—a useless assignment, everyone knew, but they had to be given something to do as the long days passed. Still, he hadn't minded it today. It gave him a chance to think, and he desperately needed to do some thinking.

He hadn't made much progress, however, by the time Samish had dismissed him and the worst part of the day began.

He walked slowly down the central stairway, down to the lowest level of the Ship, where most of the rest of the crew were already seated around the golden machine. He walked over to his own seat opposite Sabbata, who lowered her head in greeting. They did not speak.

Rothra was in charge today, as usual looking tired and out of sorts. "All right," he said, "let's hurry it up. I'm sick of giving bad reports about this, so let's do a little better tonight, shall we?" He walked over to the machine, which, like the Ship, was a pyramid in shape, and pressed a button at its base. It hummed slightly and turned a dull copper color. "All right, let's go," he snapped, striding back to the edge of the room.

Tenon looked at Sabbata. Her eyes were on him for a moment, then they closed. His closed too.

There was nothing for a moment, and then the struggle: the probing, the adjustment, the stabs of anger and frustration, wills stretched taut over the void. Tenon knew what was happening outside: the crew couples hunched over, straining together, the *retheo* changing from copper to red and almost to white (he knew why it was *almost* white), Rothra glaring impatiently at it and them. And he knew

46

what was happening inside himself as well: nothing. Sabbata's efforts were becoming sporadic, perfunctory. There was a haze of sadness and hurt perplexity over everything. It cannot be helped, he thought, drifting, drifting away. It cannot be helped.

All right, all right, that's enough—thoughts or words? Words. "All right, let it go," Rothra repeated as their eyes opened. "Just as bad as ever. You people'd better straighten out or we'll never get home." The *retheo* was back to the copper color. He walked up to it again and turned it off. "That's it. Up to the service. You better pray you do this right before very long."

The crew members got up and headed for the stairs.

Sabbata and Tenon walked together, in silence, up to the second level, and into the oval-shaped Room of the Ancients. They took their accustomed seats and waited along with the other restless crew members.

Tenon tried to think of something to say. "Whose rite is it today?" he asked Sabbata.

She gave him an a-lot-it-matters-to-you stare, then softened and said, "Ascanth, I think. It's hard to keep track, for some reason, with this new day-length."

"Why couldn't we stay on our own time, and let the aliens adjust to us?" Tenon wondered.

"Zanla," she replied, as if that were all the explanation that was needed.

Zanla, he repeated to himself, and he could feel his body become tense with fear. "He's late," he remarked, struggling to seem normal (as if that were possible with Sabbata).

"He and Ergentil are probably having another fight."

"But the Departure is set. What else is there to fight about?"

"They'll find something. They wouldn't be happy otherwise." Sabbata looked at him meaningfully. He turned away.

When Ergentil finally appeared she looked weary and cross—like Rothra; like all of them. She was wearing her white vestments. She surveyed the room quickly, motioned behind her, and entered, followed by Zanla.

They took their positions at the two foci of the ellipse.

The crew members stood. The lights dimmed, except for flickering illumination on Zanla and Ergentil. A low moaning music arose from beneath them. It swirled through the room for a while, sighed, and faded. The crew clattered back into their seats.

Ergentil's arms were raised in front of her, palms up. "On this day we honor the memory of Ascanth Most Sage. We seek the blessing of his wisdom on our endeavors. We seek to know what is good for our people, as he knew. We seek to understand what he was the first to perceive. Let us seek his wisdom." Her palms turned down, and she spread her arms out to encompass the room. The crew bowed their heads.

Tenon sneaked a look at Sabbata. Her eyes were shut tight in a fair pretense of meditation. Was she really trying to reach Ascanth's wisdom? He doubted it. It was a sham; they all knew it, but they were locked into it. And it would take Chitlan to set them free, to let them worship the true essence of life instead of some dried-up ghost that no longer had the power to move them.

Zanla was preparing for the reading, leafing through the Chronicles of the Ancients to find his place. Ergentil stared at him sourly. "I read from the Chronicle of Ascanth," he recited finally. "Pay heed to the greatness of our past.

"Now the people did not understand why man and woman both had to be a part of the sacred machines. So the Elders brought the question to Ascanth, who strove to answer them in these words:

" 'Man by himself is nothing. Woman by herself is nothing. But together they are life itself. Life by itself is little. Machines by themselves are less. But together they are in command of all-that-is. With man and *retheo* we go one step, with woman and *retheo* we go another step, with man, woman, and *retheo* we cross the Universe.'

"And someone asked if it made a difference which man and which woman, and Ascanth replied:

" 'Could we cross the Universe in a sailboat? Just as the machine makes a difference, the people make a difference. An unclean person and a broken machine will produce much the same result. The only difference is that it is easier to fix a *retheo* than it is to fix a person.' "

And on it went, the same old dreary, meaningless platitudes. Where had they all led? he could remember the Disciple Argal asking. Had the endless series of Ships increased the happiness or the goodness of the people? Had all the rules and rituals done anything but perpetuate a system that oppressed the planet, that chose to ignore the truth sprouting all around it like buds in springtime?

Tenon had difficulty containing his impatience as they plodded through the Litany of Praise. It had been tolerable when it was just a mindless formality—something your family had done generation after generation, like bowing in thanks to the ground before eating your supper. But now there was something in its place, and each day it seemed harder to mimic the appropriate responses, to act like a devout Numian when he knew that they would put him to death if they found out what he truly believed.

After the Litany more music, and then the Act of Homage—always the worst part. In silence, starting with the youngest, they trudged up—first to Zanla, then to Ergentil—sank to the floor in front of each, and murmured *"Alm a Numos."* Tenon lived in fear that his unbelief would become so obvious that the Master and the Priestess could not help but recognize it as they gazed down at him.

Tonight he need not have worried. Neither was paying any attention to him, or to any of the rest of the crew. They were acting out their parts as much as he was. How could he give homage to people like this?

Tenon picked himself up, returned to his seat, and waited until the rest were through for the Dismissal.

"May the words and deeds of the Ancients illumine our lives," Ergentil said, and turned to Zanla.

"Well," Zanla said to them, "you've had a tough day I know, and we've all been under a lot of pressure, so I won't keep you long. Just remember that it was the wisdom of people like Ascanth that brought us to where we are today. If we can all strive to have a tenth of his wisdom we will make the most of our opportunity and prepare for an even more glorious future. All right, you are dismissed."

The lights came up, and Zanla and Ergentil left quickly. "If I hear him say 'an even more glorious future' one more time I think I'll be sick," someone behind Tenon muttered.

They all followed the Master and Priestess out of the oval room, and headed down to the refectory.

At dinner the favorite topic of conversation was, as always, Departure. What is the first thing you'll do when you get back? The first meal, the first bath, the first *cumoli* concert, the first orgy . . . they would all be heroes when they returned, and for once in their lives all pleasures (within the bounds of Numian propriety) would be accessible to them.

"I'll sit in the front row at the Turquoise Hill and watch the *touvon* dancers spin their patterns by moonlight. And they'll spin one around me, faster and faster, till the world is just a blur of color and dance. . . ."

"Yes, but first a bath. They say you're allowed to bathe in the marble tubs at the Council Palace, and the bath maidens are the most beautiful in all of Numos. . . ."

"But imagine going home. Just riding into town alone, say, as if nothing had happened, and wandering into the wineshop and laying down a goldpiece . . ."

"They say the ceremony in the *golossi* is something, especially if you've been out near the maximum. Imagine what it will be like after this Voyage? Remember when we were leaving, the crowd sitting there in silence—more people than I ever . . ."

Tenon felt as if he were being suffocated. He nibbled at his food for a while, then excused himself. He could feel Sabbata's gaze on him as he left the room.

She came in to him later, as he lay in darkness in their small cubicle. She turned on a light and sat opposite him, just staring at him for a while. "This is serious," she said finally.

He didn't reply.

"The problem with the *retheo*—it's us," she went on. "You've locked me out. It's all wrong, all off-center. We have to see Ergentil—"

"I will not see Ergentil."

"This can't go on much longer."

He gestured his agreement slackly.

She continued to stare at him, as if sight could provide understanding where words failed. After a few moments she gave up. "Mal and Osha are playing *distangi* tonight. They invited us in. Will you come?"

"No. I'm sorry."

"Very well."

She left immediately, and Tenon felt nothing but relief.

He was scared. The Disciple Argal had said that much would be demanded of him, but he hadn't expected so much, so soon. He still had difficulty comprehending that it wasn't a reprimand he was risking, or dismissal, but death. Cold, final death. He knew that that wasn't right, of course. Death, in his new religion, was a glorious beginning, especially when you died *for* the religion. But old emotions die hard, and he couldn't escape his fear.

He had done right. He knew that. He had seen an opportunity and he had taken it. But in the first flush of his enthusiasm and wonder he hadn't thought through the consequences. Now he had.

Angela would try to help him, and she would succeed. He was sure of that. It was part of the pattern, of the *vomurd*. The Earthpeople would make demands of Zanla, and Zanla would—what?

Zanla would realize that they could only have found out about Chitlan from a crew member. He would do everything in his power to discover that crew member. He would succeed.

It would hardly require any work at all. Especially if Sabbata were to see it as her duty to tell about their problem. And that would be it. Perhaps Zanla would wait until they returned to Numos to carry out the punishment. Probably not.

Tenon turned on his stomach and listened to his breathing. In, out. In, out. They strangled heretics.

He had not wanted to come. He had known it would be difficult—although not this difficult. But it was unheard of to refuse. He would have been placed immediately under suspicion. Argal had urged him to go. "We have no need of more martyrs," he said. "We need you where you are."

But they didn't need him anymore, surely. He had

played his part, and what happened to him now mattered little. In a way he should feel free now. Free of all that bound him, free to worship Chitlan, free to be what Chitlan wanted him to be.

A sudden excitement filled him, not unlike the excitement he had felt upon first hearing of Chitlan. He wanted to jump, to shout, to run. But he did none of those things. Instead he just lay in darkness, waiting. Endless hours, changing his mind a hundred times, but finally he was sure, determined, eager.

The door opened and he could feel once again Sabbata's questioning gaze upon him. He did not move. He heard the rustle of her preparation for bed, and then she was lying next to him. Her hand tentatively stroked his back, but when there was no response she turned away.

He waited. Her breathing became regular, but still he waited, imagining the crew straggling back to their rooms after their evening's pleasures, falling asleep, dreaming of home. He waited. Then, silently, gently, he rose. He felt for and found his light jacket in the corner of his closet, and walked out into the corridor.

It was deserted. Quickly he headed to his right until he reached the large door that led to the stairwell. He opened it a crack and slid through. Then up one level, another, two steps at a time. At the landing he paused to catch his breath, and to consider what he should do.

There was no plan. If he had to fight, he would fight. This corridor would be deserted too—and the rooms as well. The officers would all be up on the first level. If the fight was not too loud, he would have a chance.

He moved out into the corridor. It was dimly lit at night. Good. He felt a thrill of guilt and fear as he passed by Zanla's office. But there was no one there. Only at the end of the corridor, at his goal. He walked silently toward it.

He was not big; surprise would be his only advantage. He hoped it was not someone he knew well: the struggle would be all the more difficult then. A few paces away he stopped, and tensed. The guard would be in the small room to his left. He would be looking the other way. He would not expect it.

Tenon leaped toward the room. And just managed to

stop himself at the door. The guard stirred but did not waken. "*Vomurd*," Tenon said to himself. He walked past the guard and slid open the portal to another world.

In the first instant he was half inclined to turn back. This world was dark, and confusing, and bitter cold. How could he hope to find refuge in it? But of course he had come too far to turn back. He shut the door behind him, and started carefully down the long staircase to the ground.

They had guards too, of course, but they too were looking the other way, more interested in keeping Earthpeople away from the ship than Numoi away from Earth. He crouched low to the stairs as he descended, and prayed that the helmeted creatures at the bottom would not turn around.

They didn't. Five steps from the bottom Tenon leaped over the railing and landed silently beside the stairs. He looked around. There were no other guards nearby that he could see. He moved to his right until he was well outside the guards' line of sight, and then he walked slowly away from the ship.

The area around it was deserted. Who could be outside in this cold? It was very well lit, however, and he felt conspicuous. He picked up his pace, and soon he was in the shadows of a building. He could hear the murmur of voices inside. It was probably warm in there; he longed to join the voices. But would they protect him? No, he needed a sign: something to show him that the *vomurd* was continuing. He walked on.

And before very long he reached a fence, long and high and fiercely metallic. He could see a guard to his left, but once again the man was facing away from the Ship. Well then, he must climb the fence.

It was difficult for his hands to get a grip, and at the top were twisted strands of wire that tore at his flesh; but it was all right, he should be able to put up with pain. When he reached the ground on the other side he stopped to look back through the fence at the large pyramid that was his past, and then he trudged off along the road he found at his feet.

Around him were dark, looming hills, and tall, hard, bare-looking plants. Over everything was a layer of crusted snow. He had never actually seen snow before, but there was plenty of it in the land of the Stani, and Argal had spoken of it more than once. White grains of ice, as far as you could see. He shivered, and looked up at the alien sky. The stars were sharp and clear, their strange patterns almost as unsettling as the snow. Was one of them *their* star? He was unclear on such matters. Did anyone really know? It didn't matter now.

By the fence he had seen a few of those fast-moving mechanical vehicles other crew members had talked about in tones of wonder, but none were on this road. Perhaps they were not used at night. Perhaps no one was allowed out after dark. There was so much he didn't know—including how much farther he had to walk before he would find what he was looking for. So far there was nothing—no sign of a village, a farmhouse, a light. He could be going entirely in the wrong direction—a town just out of sight behind him, none for a day's travel ahead of him. They would find his frozen body in the snow, by the road, and they would say: a fit punishment for a Chitlanian, to die in a land like the Stani's.

If he was not used to the cold, at least he was used to the walking. He had had enough forced marches to keep his legs in shape, even after the inactivity of the voyage: rushing to the border to subdue some recalcitrant tribe, providing an escort for some minor ambassador, scouring the hillside for heretics . . .

He recalled that painstaking search, knowing only that they were looking for enemies of the state, going from cave to cave, sword at the ready, determined to root out the traitors.

And he was the one who found them; scrambling up a small slope at dusk, weary and frustrated, he had entered the low cave and shined his torch, and there they were. About twenty of them, white-robed, gentle-eyed, sitting, waiting. His sword came out, and then he was calling for assistance, and one of the white-robes had said: "Calm yourself, soldier. You have nothing to fear from us." And they came with him peacefully, praying all the while to Someone he had not yet heard of.

He had received a promotion for his daring single-

handed capture of the heretics. The promotion had made
him eligible for the Voyage. But that meant nothing to him
compared with the image in his memory of those faces as
they went to their deaths, faces transfigured by an emotion
he had never felt, but longed to feel. Soon after that he was
scouring the hills, alone, looking for someone who trusted
him enough to bring him to Argal.

His hands were numb. He clapped them against his side
to bring the feeling back. He was having difficulty focus-
ing his eyes. He had to squint continually to keep them
working. His ears roared with pain. His legs wanted to
stop, but stopping, he now realized, meant death.

And besides, there were signs now of life: lights in the
hills, a dwelling, then, after a while, another. He squinted
at each dwelling as he passed it. Not what he was looking
for. Not yet.

Millions, he kept telling himself. There are millions.

One of the vehicles suddenly appeared, its lights like
some incredible animal eyes piercing the darkness. He
stopped, transfixed, as it roared past him, its occupant
faceless behind the glare of the lights. He took a deep
breath, and continued.

He had been a soldier all his life, and yet he had never
known fear. Occasionally there would be danger, but the
Numoi were always in control, and besides, to die for Numos (so he had believed) was the greatest possible glory of
your life.

Now he would gladly die for Chitlan, but still he was
afraid, because he was alone in the dark on a strange
world, and he did not know what hazards awaited him
around the corner, over the next rise, and he did not want
to die senselessly, by walking on the wrong side of the
road, or touching an object that was not supposed to be
touched, or making a sound where silence was required.

He did not know whether the water in his eyes was
caused by the cold, or by something else.

He did not want to think of the past anymore, but he
couldn't help it, to keep his thoughts in this world was to
invite despair; and if he lost the will to keep his legs moving then everything would have been in vain.

He thought of Argal, who had walked the length of Numos, and all the outlands as well, risking his life with every step he took. But he had a mission, and he never complained. He thrived on it, really: how he would have enjoyed the challenge of this situation.

Tenon pictured Argal sitting in a hearthchamber, his dirty peasant robes gathered around him, his face creased and scarred with the ravages of his life. And the eyes! Eyes that held knowledge and truth, that had pierced deeper into the mysteries of all-that-is than any living being. Eyes, Tenon thought, with a shiver, that he would never look into again.

He recalled the first time: they had led Tenon to him blindfolded, at night, wary of a pure-blooded soldier with an impeccable record. He kept waiting for the feel of a knife against his throat, but these people were different (he kept reminding himself); that was why he had put himself in their hands.

When the blindfold came off he found himself in the stone-floored hearthchamber of a peasant farmhouse. In the dim firelight he saw a couple of young rustics regarding him suspiciously and, beyond, the foreigner he had struggled so long to meet, the foreigner who had a price of five thousand goldpieces on his head.

"Come and sit, soldier," Argal had said in a low, friendly voice. "Perhaps we can learn from each other."

But what could he teach Argal? He knew only what the Numian schools had taught him, and that, it turned out, was less than nothing in Argal's eyes.

For some reason Argal spoke little of Chitlan that first night. Perhaps he wanted to tear down Tenon's old religion before building a new one; perhaps it was just where his thoughts were when Tenon arrived. At any rate, he began by speaking of the Ancients.

"It is fascinating to me how little even educated Numoi know about these Ancients. It's nothing more than myth and pious double-talk—which, you know, is precisely what the Ancients wanted. Did you know, for example, that there were exiles from Numos at the time the Ancients were putting together the *hasali* you are now a part of?"

Tenon, of course, had not known that.

"Some of them reached the land of the Stani. They

wrote about what they understood—and feared—but they were foreigners and, I'm afraid, they were at best ignored, at worst mistreated. Their writings lay unread—until I came upon them. I was just a young scholar back then, and I had not even heard of Chitlan. So the Stani leaders threw open their archives to me, not knowing what they possessed."

"What was it?" Tenon asked, intrigued and half afraid.

"Well," Argal replied, "here is my interpretation of it. I believe it to be true. You see, the Ancients were practical, clear-sighted, and, according to their lights, benevolent people who above all were interested in answering one question: how do you set up a lasting, peaceful civilization? You will not find this question discussed in the Chronicles of the Ancients, or any of the other writings that have been preserved by the priestesses, because all mention of it had to be suppressed as part of the answer."

"And what was their answer?"

"Oh, there were many parts to it, like the structure of the government and the size of the nation. But the centerpiece was this: to create a religion. And the centerpiece of the religion was the Ship."

"But isn't—wasn't—?"

"Isn't the Ship proof of the truth of your religion? No, it is only proof of the genius of the Ancients. I don't pretend to understand how it works, but I do know there is nothing miraculous about it—nothing to compare, for example, with a resurrection from the dead. But we will come to that another night.

"You see, they wanted it to *appear* miraculous. So they destroyed all documents concerning the theory of timeless travel and the construction of the Ship. They cloaked their work in mystical terminology, and taught their successors how to copy what they had done, but not how to understand it. Instead of using what they had learned to add to the material well-being of their nation, they used it to transform its spirit.

"They gave Numos a central symbol, a ceaseless quest that would provide a focus for all the work and thoughts of its people. They were lucky, I think, in a couple of points. Enough of the Ships returned from the black void that they have not come to symbolize utter futility. And the crews never have discovered other intelligent life—because that would end the quest, and with it the value of the symbol."

(Tenon-by-the-hearth had circled his hand slowly in understanding, finally getting used to this strange perspective on his world, starting the slow transformation that would lead him far from his mindless orthodoxy. Tenon-in-the-cold-alien-air, product of the transformation, thought: the Voyages are too important to Numos, though. The Council will simply redefine the goal, and the Voyages will continue, more meaningless than ever. But that has nothing to do with me anymore. Tenon shivered, and tried to walk faster.)

Argal's eyes had gleamed in the firelight, pleased at Tenon's understanding. "Do you see?" he exclaimed. "It is an artificial religion, designed to provide stability and meaning to a civilization. As such it has been successful and, in some ways, I grant, admirable. *But it is not the truth.* A civilization, it seems, can be based on a lie, but now we know the truth, and the truth will destroy this civilization like a rock shattering a hollow, decayed fossil."

Tenon noticed one of the young peasants writing down Argal's words, and he started to realize that this was the beginning of something immense, that he was hearing words that would be remembered in a thousand generations the way the acts of the Ancients were remembered in his. But still there were doubts. "If a lie is so powerful, how will the truth destroy it?"

"Its time has come," Argal responded. "The lie is not what it once was. The crews still go off every twenty cycles to meet their fate, but there is confusion and fear beneath their brave façades. The priestesses still carry out the prescribed rituals, but there is boredom behind their gestures. The Council still rules, but the people feel free to grumble at their edicts. The entire planet is ready to listen, ready to believe. And that is precisely why Chitlan chose this moment to appear in our midst. We will be victorious, and there is not a power in the Universe that can stop us."

And how often had he heard those words spoken—by different hearths, to other new believers? Yet they never failed to thrill him. Often he lacked Argal's utter certainty in the final triumph, but he never lacked faith in him, or in Chitlan.

A cold wind cut through him, as he realized again that Argal was gone. He was on his own; he had left those hearths behind forever.

There were dwellings all around him now, but no sign of what he was looking for. Pray, he must pray. His legs must continue to move, he must fight off the tears. . . .

And eventually he saw it—sharply etched against the planet's bright half-moon, just as he had imagined it. Angela's words echoed in his mind: they put Him to death on a cross. And she herself had worn a tiny gold cross around her neck. Symbol of her faith.

O, lucky people, who could display their symbols so openly! He rushed over the banks of snow to the building with the cross, joy and anticipation warming his frigid body. Across the walk, up the short flight of stairs . . .

And the door was locked. Tenon stared at it in disbelief. That could not be. Then he reasoned: not everyone on the planet was a follower of Jesus. Perhaps there were still people who wanted to harm them. Of course they would lock their place of worship in that case. But certainly their chief priest or priestess would be inside—asleep, most likely, but eager to help a believer in trouble.

He pounded on the door. No one came. He pounded again. His hands, already cut and raw from the wire of the fence, ached with the effort, but the door remained locked. Finally he gave up and started to walk around the building, looking for other entrances. They were all locked. There were windows, of course. He could break a window and get inside. But that would be desecration. That would not be allowed.

He came around to the front again and sat on the steps, exhausted and fearful. Perhaps someone would open it up in the morning. But when was morning? He could not survive much longer without shelter. How much worse a death that would be—frozen on the very steps of their temple, his goal reached but meaningless.

That could not happen. He struggled to think things through. It was clear that he had to get indoors. There were plenty of dwellings. Most of them were probably occupied. What he needed was one occupied by a follower of Jesus. But how would he know?

He would have to take a chance. Which one?

The one nearest the temple, obviously. Would someone who was not a follower of Jesus want to live next to one of His temples?

Tenon got up and walked across a short pathway to the nearest dwelling. It was in darkness, like the temple. He stood in front of the door for a long time, summoning his courage. It had to be done, he told himself. There was no other way. He knocked.

And knocked. And after an eternity a light appeared behind the door. He saw the shadow of a person through the small, curtained glass panes and heard a brief, gruff sentence. There was nothing he could say, so he knocked some more.

Finally the door opened a crack—still locked with a chain—and a face appeared.

They looked at each other through the crack, and Tenon dimly realized that the man was as frightened as he was.

With his trembling hands Tenon tried to form a cross. "Jesus," he whispered, hoping it sounded right on his alien tongue. "Jesus."

The man kept looking at him, and the chain remained in place, and suddenly Tenon could take no more, and the tears came streaming out of his eyes. "Jesus," he moaned as he felt his legs giving way, and then he heard the chain move, and the door swung open, and he fell forward into warmth and light.

8

Father Gardner, in pajamas and ratty bathrobe, looked relieved and grateful. "Thanks, Al, I didn't know—I wouldn't have—"

"Of course, Ed. This is serious business. Who'd you steal that bathrobe from?"

He smiled and led Bernardi down to the kitchen.

The alien was sitting against the radiator, a blanket around his shoulders, his bandaged hands clasping a cup of tea. He stared at the two men as they stood in the doorway.

"His hands were kind of cut up," Gardner said. "I did what I could."

"He looks frightened," Bernardi noted. "And human."

"He likes tea," Gardner remarked.

Bernardi walked over to the huddled figure. "Tenon?" he asked.

The alien put down his cup and moved his hand quickly in a circle.

"I think that means he agrees with you," Gardner said from across the room.

Bernardi pointed to himself. "Al Bernardi." Then he put out his hand.

Tenon grasped it with both of his. "Albernardi," he repeated. Then he withdrew his hands, formed them into a cross, and pointed inquiringly at Bernardi.

Bernardi nodded vigorously, thought for a moment, and spun his hand in a circle.

Tenon's eyes lit up and he too spun his hand.

"It's the latest dance," Bernardi said to Gardner.

"I'm glad you're both having a good time," Gardner replied. "But what are we going to do with him, Al?"

Bernardi looked down at Tenon and considered. "Well, I

61

guess he's escaped from the ship, probably because they found out about his religion. So presumably they'll want him back. But do we want to let them take him?"

"He can't stay here," Gardner interjected hurriedly. "I've got a parish to run. I can't—"

Bernardi waved him silent. He walked over and leaned back against the sink. Tenon's eyes followed him. Did he understand what they were talking about?

"If we send him back, Ed, they'll kill him."

"But if we keep him, we're liable to get arrested or something. Why do we have to make that decision?"

Bernardi thought for a moment and nodded slowly. "You're right. So let's call the Vatican." He fished in his pocket and pulled out a scrap of paper. There was a wall phone next to the door. He went over to it, punched a few numbers, talked to an operator, and punched a few more. "What time do you figure it is in Rome?" he asked as the connection was made. Father Gardner shrugged helplessly.

Collingwood answered in Italian. He sounded sleepy.

"Anthony, it's Bernardi. From America. We have a complication."

"What's that?" The voice was instantly alert.

"Our friend from the ship has escaped. He's sitting with us in the rectory kitchen at Most Precious Blood."

"How the hell did he manage that?"

"Beats me. It also beats me how he ended up here, but he did. So now what?"

There was a long silence as the problem crossed the ocean. "If we hold onto him," Collingwood said finally, "it will probably force everything out into the open. Clement will have to take a stand."

"That's pretty risky, though."

"True, but if we give him back we're just washing our hands of the whole business."

"So you say keep him?"

Another silence. "Can you do it?"

Bernardi shrugged. "We'll have to go into hiding. I might—"

"Don't tell me," Collingwood interrupted. "I don't want to know. Let's keep the Vatican as clean in this as possible."

"Fine by me. But look—if I'm out hiding with him on my own, I'm going to stay hiding until I get the message otherwise. From the Pope."

"Right. Until Clement gives the word."

Bernardi smiled. "Hey, Tony? I'm a little surprised at you. Isn't your neck sticking out a bit far on this?"

There was a slight pause. "I've been known to consider the good of the Church, Al," Collingwood replied.

"Well, I approve. See you who knows when."

"Right. Good luck, then."

"Thanks. I'll need it."

Bernardi hung up. The adrenaline was pumping already. He felt great.

"You're going to take him?" Gardner asked.

"Sure. Wanna come along?"

"No thanks. Where will you go?"

"You don't want to know."

"That's true."

Bernardi looked over at Tenon, whose eyes were fixed on them. His tea mug was empty. "You think he's warm enough to take a trip?"

"I guess so. I'll lend him a coat. Are you going back to the residence first?"

"No, I think we'll just disappear into the night."

"They won't like you taking their car."

Bernardi laughed. "We all have to make sacrifices. Get that coat, will you? People may already be looking for him."

Car. That's what Albernardi called it. His vocabulary was increasing. Grammar was the hard part, though. He had heard them talking about that on the ship. Only Ergentil seemed to have any idea how to put the words together.

But now he knew this was a *car*, and he blessed it, because it was taking him far from the ship. He was streaking through the night, warm and secure, with a friend by his side. It was unbelievable, but he had succeeded. For the first time in a long while he began to relax. The hum of the *car* was so nice. He closed his eyes and listened to the hum.

* * *

The darkness was changing almost imperceptibly into predawn fog. He would have to hurry. They rose at some ungodly hour, and he would prefer to be seen by as few people as possible. Even them.

When he was a couple of miles away, Bernardi stopped at a roadside phone. He looked over at Tenon. Still asleep. He got out and made his call.

The phone rang several times, and Bernardi began to think the whole thing wasn't such a hot idea. Then there was a click and an alert hello, and Bernardi explained his situation as quickly and as vaguely as he could. The response was brief and affirmative, so he got back in the car and headed for the place.

There was a rutted country road, then a long, winding drive up a rocky hill. Not a pleasant route in fog and darkness, with little sleep. If he missed the road, he could get them both killed. A strange way to go.

But he made it to the top. He stopped the car at the far end of the empty parking area. He looked at Tenon again. Best to wake him this time. No telling what he would do if he woke by himself here.

Tenon looked baffled for a moment when he opened his eyes. Bernardi couldn't be sure he got his message across with his gestures, but Tenon seemed to understand, and stayed where he was when Bernardi walked away from the car.

Bernardi strode quickly up to the front door of the building and gazed in. With a sigh of relief he saw the gray-fringed bald head of his friend, sitting in a chair reading a book. Bernardi rapped softly on the glass door. The man looked up, smiled, and let him in. "Well, what in the world are you up to, Albert?" the man whispered.

"A long story, Michael. I'm sorry if I got you up."

"Oh, nonsense. I rise at two."

Bernardi shook his head. "I wouldn't last a day with you guys. May I—?"

"Of course. Come into my office. I have a feeling great favors are going to be asked of me."

"Oh no, no. Just advice."

They both smiled.

Bernardi sat opposite Michael in his sparsely furnished office and told him the story from the beginning.

"Quite exciting," Michael commented at the end, in the voice of one whom nothing excited. "I guess I can see where it's all heading. And now you want my advice."

Bernardi smiled.

"My advice is for you to leave immediately and go far away. Chances are they will track you down, you know."

"I see what you mean. And you?"

Michael shrugged. "Our lives are very peaceful. Nothing happens here."

"Lucky you." Bernardi arose. "Time to be going, then."

"I'll see you to your car."

Bernardi walked back outside, with Michael following. Dawn was clearly approaching now, and with it some promise of warmth after the long night. Tenon was still sitting in the car, huddled in Father Gardner's coat. "Will you introduce me?" Michael asked.

"Of course."

They laughed, and Bernardi performed the amenities. Then Michael grasped Bernardi's hand. "Good luck, Albert. It may be dangerous."

"Oh well. It's about time I had a little danger in my life."

Michael looked at him. "I do believe you're enjoying this."

Bernardi looked back. "Aren't *you?*"

They laughed again, and then turned back to Tenon.

9

Sabbata awoke shivering. She had never felt such cold. It was beyond discomfort, beyond pain. It was killing her. She instinctively reached out for Tenon. . . .

But Tenon wasn't there.

And then her mind started to sort things out. It wasn't *her* feeling, it was a bonding feeling; sometimes powerful emotions or sensations leaked across, even unconsciously. She must have been dreaming of Tenon, and slipped into the familiar routine while still asleep. It was Tenon's coldness, then. He was somewhere in the cold.

He had left the Ship.

Sabbata willed the bonding away, and the coldness retreated to the fringes of her mind. Her normal feelings flooded in to take its place, and she began to cry. How could he leave the Ship? That was not only forbidden, it was unthinkable. He was disappearing into the alien world, and leaving her behind.

Her body began to produce its own coldness.

There was supposed to be such a depth of feeling between you and your bondmate. It was inevitable, they said. But Tenon had always been so distant, so uninterested. They had worked together all right until the Voyage, but then things had deteriorated until there was nothing: no bond, only the weight of his mind, resisting. She should have told someone right away, before the Voyage, but that would have meant she couldn't go, and she kept hoping it would change, that she could *make* Tenon respond.

But now her bed was empty, and she had to decide what to do.

Zanla had to be told. Should she go up there now, awaken him, tell him everything? No, she couldn't bring herself to do that. What if she were wrong? What if there had been a duty change that Tenon hadn't bothered to tell her about? What if Zanla had sent him on some kind of secret mission? It was all so confusing. She would wait, she decided finally. If he had not returned by worktime, she would speak to Zanla.

Worktime. Sabbata was not used to being on the third level, particularly this early in the morning. She looked nervously up and down the corridor, expecting Samish to appear and reprimand her. She wished with all her heart that she didn't have to be here, but there was no avoiding it now. Tenon was gone, and it was her duty to report it.

When Zanla finally approached, she had to suppress an urge to flee. He looked surprised, of course, a trifle uncertain. She bowed deeply. "*Alm a Numos.*"

"*Alm a Numos*, Sabbata. What, uh, brings you up here?"

"Master, Tenon—my bondmate—I think he's gone."

"Gone?"

"Left the Ship," she managed to whisper.

Zanla stared at her for a long moment, then opened the door of his office. "Come inside," he commanded.

She followed him in. She had never seen the Master's office before. She barely saw it now, as she concentrated on the details of her story. She went through all of it, everything she should have told before, everything she thought might matter now.

At the end Zanla was silent for a while, looking down at the table in front of him. "You felt cold last night," he said finally. "Any bonding feelings now?"

She searched. "Nothing. He could be asleep or—"

"Or unconscious. Or dead."

"Or the bond could just be broken," she added, unwilling to consider those possibilities.

Zanla gestured slackly in agreement. "All right, then. Why? Why would he act like this?"

The question was familiar to Sabbata. She had been asking herself the same one for a long time. Her answer was strange and frightening, but it was all she could think of. "I think . . . he may be a disciple of Chitlan."

"You think? Have you any proof?"

"I only know that this should be the greatest opportunity in the life of a citizen of Numos," she replied. "And Tenon scorned it. I feel he must have had some other *hasali*. Otherwise . . ." She could not finish.

Zanla pondered her answer, then motioned wearily to the door. "Go get Samish," he said. "We will search the Ship, just to be sure."

She bowed in obedience and rose. "Master?" she asked hesitantly, afraid to bring this last question up.

"Yes?"

"What will happen to me, Master? Without my bondmate—"

"Oh, don't worry," Zanla said, trying to be cheerful. "It's not your fault. We still have the power to return, even if we don't get Tenon back. But we *will* get him back."

Sabbata should have been reassured by the last sentence, but somehow Zanla's tone frightened her more than ever. She bowed again, and hurried off to find Samish. It was out of her hands now.

The search was quickly completed, and Samish stood in front of Zanla, awaiting further instructions. "Get last night's exit guard and have him questioned," Zanla ordered. "If he was asleep, relieve him of his duties. Tell the Earth guards that all meetings are canceled for today and that I wish to see Bacquier immediately."

"Yes, Master," Samish replied. "Priestess Ergentil—"

"And keep Ergentil away from me, will you?" he snapped.

Samish bowed and scurried away.

All he needed now was to have Ergentil carping at him, Zanla thought. He had to have time to plan before he confronted Bacquier, and she would only draw him into a fruitless argument over who was to blame, only point out the consequences that were already all too apparent to him.

You've taken too many risks, he could hear her say. We should have left as soon as we discovered the planet had intelligent inhabitants. Let the Council decide how—or whether—to deal with these creatures. Now see what has happened. Now look at the chaos you've created.

But they were necessary risks, Zanla thought, unconsciously slipping into a mental debate with her. Isn't the purpose of these Voyages to find another intelligent race? And after generations of fruitless searching, are we to leave the race behind the instant we find it, with the possibility that the *retheo* setting was incorrect, or that a comet will strike, and we will never find it again? What is my job for, if not to—

He noticed Samish standing in front of him. "The guards say that Bacquier will be coming shortly, Master."

"Did they seem surprised when you called off the meetings?" Zanla inquired.

Samish considered. "I don't know. They asked me why, but—"

He didn't need to complete the answer. Zanla understood. How can you interpret their gestures, expressions, words, when you have no referents, when you're not even sure they *have* the same emotions as you?

And now, Zanla knew, he had to interpret correctly. Unless Tenon was brought back immediately, Zanla would have to judge Bacquier's responses and decide if he was telling the truth. He couldn't afford to be wrong.

He waved Samish away, and tried to concentrate on the question he had to answer.

The question was: if the aliens had Tenon, what could they learn from him?

They knew so much. Numian didn't have words for most of their inventions. Zanla had only the vaguest understanding of any of them. Their science seemed almost in the realm of magic . . . yet they didn't understand timeless travel. But surely they must be capable of understanding it, surely it was a mere quirk of circumstance that Numos had it and they didn't; surely all they needed were a few clues. . . .

And what clues did Tenon possess? The techniques of bonding, of course, perhaps a few elementary notions about the *retheo*. Did he know the *retheo* settings for home, for Numos? It was not unlikely.

And if he did, and if his knowledge gave Earth scientists the key they needed, then Numos was in grave danger. These humans were energetic, and resourceful, and powerful. If they could find their way across the stars to Numos, the planet would be theirs for the taking.

Zanla shivered at the unthinkable thought. He had to get Tenon back.

"Claude Bacquier," Samish announced from the doorway.

"Send him in," Zanla said, rising in automatic politeness.

Bacquier came in, followed by the translator Colin. They bowed, and Zanla motioned to them to sit. "Thank you for coming so promptly, Claude," he began.

"Not at all," Bacquier responded to the translation. "I am, of course, eager to know what is the matter, so that we can do what is necessary and the meetings can continue."

Zanla studied Bacquier's face for signs of deception. But in addition to being an alien Bacquier was a diplomat, trained to impassivity. There was nothing to be seen. Zanla plunged ahead. "One of our crew members is missing. He left the Ship last night. We have some reason to believe he is a member of an illegal religious sect and might have escaped to avoid punishment. We, of course, want him found and returned to us. We cannot continue the meetings until this is done."

Bacquier inclined his head slightly at the end of the translation, paused, and then began speaking rapidly. "I am very sorry to hear about this. Certainly we do not have him in our custody, but I cannot believe he escaped from the compound. A thorough search should turn him up."

"And if it doesn't?"

Bacquier shrugged his shoulders. "Then we will expand the search. How far can he have gotten?"

Zanla was somewhat reassured. Bacquier's reaction seemed so matter-of-fact and open that his worries appeared groundless. Still, he felt obliged to make the point as clear as he could. "I thank you for any help you can give us. This is a serious matter for us, you must understand. Everything else must wait until it is settled."

"We will do all that we can. Now, if you could give us some sort of description . . ."

Zanla did his best, and Bacquier departed. His search— if he made one—took much longer than Samish's, but the result was the same. He returned early in the afternoon to report that no progress had been made.

"This distresses me greatly," Zanla said.

"It distresses me too," Bacquier replied. "I hope you do not think that the United Nations had any part in your crew member's disappearance."

"I have no way of knowing one way or the other, do I? All I know is that your innocence will be proved by Tenon's return."

Bacquier considered for a few moments. "We will call in experts," he said finally. "We will explore all possibilities. We have no wish to jeopardize our relations with you over such a matter. I hope you will be able to recognize our good faith."

"Find him and return him, and your good faith will be obvious."

And the meeting ended stiffly, coldly. Zanla sat in his office for a while after Bacquier left, and then he went out into the third-level corridor. What did he want now? Food? Rest? Lilorn and Sudmeta were talking at the far end of the corridor. They looked over at him but said nothing. All of them knew, of course; and they were all probably glad they weren't the ones who had to deal with the problem.

That is why I am a Master, he thought. He walked quickly up to his room on the first level. Ergentil was waiting for him there.

Her presence was a breach of etiquette, but there was little to be done about that. A Master takes conditions as he finds them, his teacher Elial had always stressed—not, however, referring to situations like this. He inclined his head slightly to acknowledge her presence.

"This is a mess," Ergentil said.

Zanla made a half-gesture of agreement.

"What are you going to do?"

Zanla went over and sat on his bed. "Rest," he said.

"Resting won't get Tenon back."

"What will?"

She didn't respond. After a pause she said, "They have him, you know. How could he avoid being caught? He'll tell them what he knows, and the one advantage we have over them will be gone."

"I know the consequences as well as you," he responded wearily. "The *possible* consequences."

"The Council won't dismiss them as *possible* consequences," Ergentil countered. "An aggressive, intelligent alien race with timeless travel, with knowledge of our existence, with superior weaponry, with the *retheo* setting for Numos . . ."

"It took the Ancients many years to build the first Ship."

"These people can send images of themselves around their planet, they have machines that fly, they—"

"All right," Zanla shouted. "I agreed it was a mess. *What do you want me to do?*"

"Leave," she said simply. "The damage has been done. We must warn the Council, we must help our scientists improve our weapons, we must prepare for war. The Earthpeople don't need anything more from us. If we stay, they will just destroy us. The Council will know nothing then. They will just assume we were lost like all the other Ships that never returned—killed by the hostile power of the Universe. Numos will be helpless. So we must go back. Now."

She was sincere, impassioned. What she said made sense. Was it because *she* said it that he didn't agree? Was it just because *he* had something to prove? He had to be careful now. Such personal matters had no place in this decision. He would have to think about it. He needed time to think. "Thank you for your advice, Ergentil," he said mildly. "I must consider it. This is a very complicated matter."

She seemed surprised at his tone. She had come prepared for a battle. "Very well," she responded uncertainly. "But time wasted only increases the danger. I will speak with you later."

"Of course." Zanla watched her leave, and lay back on the bed. He would rest first, and then think.

10

Madeleine West was writing her third report of the day when the call came. "From Washington," her secretary said in a meaningful tone.

"West speaking," she said.

"Hi Madeleine, how're things in the Big Apple?"

"Mr. Fitzgerald?" The Director was known for his informality.

"Call me Fitz, will you? Listen, are you busy?"

"Paperwork." She could never bring herself to call him Fitz.

"Yeah, I know how it is, occupational hazard. Well, I'm going to have to drag you away from it, I guess. I've got a case for you to handle. Up in Massachusetts."

"That's not my territory, sir. It could cause—"

"Yeah, well, I got orders to put my best person on this. I'll take care of any ruffled feathers."

There weren't too many people who gave Fitzgerald orders. "What kind of case is it?"

"Well, you know I can't say much over the phone. It's a missing-persons case. Sort of."

Sort of? "All right. What do you want me to do?"

"A helicopter is on its way for you. The pilot has instructions. You'll be in complete charge. Any problems, let me know. The case is all-around kind of delicate, if you know what I mean, and big shots are going to be taking an interest, so be kind of careful, okay?"

"Don't worry, Mr. Fitzgerald."

"Hey, call me Fitz."

West shoved the report aside gratefully. This sounded interesting. She was almost at the door of her office when she remembered to call her husband. "Sorry it's such short notice, but I can't make it for dinner. I just got a call."

"Well, if you have to, you have to." He sounded disappointed, but he was used to it.

"I'll call you when I can." She gave a few instructions to her secretary, and was off.

It was late afternoon by the time West arrived at the compound. She was met by a rotund French diplomat named Bacquier and a gaunt American scientist named Aronson. They were in charge. They brought her into the Holiday Inn that was headquarters for the Alien Study Team, where they were joined by a couple of faceless military people. Bacquier explained the situation to her in impeccable English.

"You see our problem," Bacquier said after he had presented the basic facts of the case. "President Gibson doesn't want it to be known that an alien is 'on the loose,' so to speak. There was enough panic when they first arrived. So we have to find him, but quietly. We have given his description to the police, but we had to say he was some sort of foreign agent, wanted for questioning."

"May I see the description?"

One of the military men shoved it over to her. She glanced at it. "Kind of vague, isn't it?"

Bacquier shrugged. "We did our best. There are constant problems of translation."

"And the aliens think you have him and are lying to them?"

"That is my impression."

"Why would they think that?"

Bacquier smiled and looked at Aronson. "Simple enough," Aronson replied. "No secret there. They don't want us to learn how they manage to travel faster than light—at least not without our paying a hefty price for the knowledge. Presumably this crew member knows something about this."

"Does that mean we'll keep him if we find him?"

Bacquier's smile broadened. Back in his department. The question was not precisely relevant, but so what? The worst he could do was refuse to answer. "I have not received any specific instructions," he replied. "My own opinion is that it would give us a short-term tactical advantage, but in the long run would be disastrous to relations between the two planets. I trust my superiors will agree with me."

"Sounds reasonable. But if this fellow is valuable, some group or country might want to kidnap him on its own—for a tactical advantage here on Earth."

"That is a possibility," Bacquier admitted. "It seems unlikely, though, that someone could breach our security, breach their security, pluck this particular fellow out of bed, and get out again. The Numoi's theory appears more reasonable to us: the fellow decided he wanted to leave for some personal reason, and so he left."

"Our security is designed to keep people *out*, not particularly to keep the aliens *in*," a white-haired general noted.

Everyone was silent, then. Waiting for her to crack the case, she supposed. Well, the way you crack it is by asking the right questions. "Is Numos a cold planet?" she asked Aronson.

"Like ours," he replied. "The Numoi live in a temperate region. Warm summers, mild winters."

"The clothing in this description doesn't sound very heavy. Is it specially insulated or something?"

"Doubt it. The few times any of them have been outside their ship they've looked pretty cold."

"How far is it to the nearest town?"

"Greenough is three miles east," a colonel answered. "But we've checked every foot of the road for twenty miles in both directions. We're scouring the woods now on either side. If he froze to death we'd have found him."

"But you haven't found him, and I can't picture him leaving the road. I suppose he could make it to Greenough, but a strange-looking person who doesn't speak any English . . . Did this fellow Tenon have any dealings with people on the staff here?"

Bacquier shook his head. "I can't imagine so. We're only allowed to speak with their officers."

"Well, he's obviously not interested in what is *allowed*. Did he have any *opportunities* for contact?"

"I don't know. Do you think someone here helped him to escape?"

West shrugged. "It's something we have to check out. Hard to see how he could still be at large without help. This is the only place for him to find help."

"Very well. I will go ask Zanla right now."

Bacquier went out into the lobby and looked around for an interpreter. None was there. He walked over to the desk. "Get me . . . uh, get me Angela Summers, please," he said to the desk clerk. Angela never minded a little extra work.

He returned to the meeting three-quarters of an hour later. "Nothing," he said. "Tenon was just some kind of support person on a lower level of the ship. Zanla doubts he ever even saw one of us."

West nodded. "So much for easy solutions. We'll just have to grind it out then. Give lie-detector tests to everyone in the compound. Conduct a house-to-house investigation in Greenough. I'll have personnel and equipment here by morning."

"Now wait," Aronson protested. "Some of the people here are among the leading scientists in the world. They won't like being subjected to a lie-detector test."

West sighed. "Too bad. I'm sure you can explain to them the necessity of it. Now if you'll excuse me, I have to make preparations. Is there a phone I can use?"

In an hour everything was ready. Fitzgerald modified slightly her plan for searching Greenough but let it go ahead because, inevitably, people had become aware that the military were searching for *someone* who had *something* to do with the aliens. "If the alien can pass for human," she argued, "we'll have all the more problems in finding him. We can't afford to cripple ourselves from the start."

Even with all this cooperation, she doubted her efforts would turn up anything. More likely, he would be found half buried in a snowbank that a bored private had somehow overlooked. The dull explanation, unfortunately, was usually the correct one. Still, she would do her part of the job. There was some satisfaction in carrying out even a useless task properly.

She still had energy left after her session on the phone, so she put her coat on and took a walk through the cold, silent compound. Like everyone, she gazed first at the brooding pyramid in its center. But unlike most, she was not awestruck or thrilled by it. She was a stubbornly earthbound person, uninterested in the cosmic questions raised by the pyramid's presence. Comparatively little interested her, actually, except for her job. Which was probably why she was so good at it, she reflected. No distractions, just her undivided attention to the case.

Of course some people saw that as a flaw, she knew. They thought she was too narrow, too demanding; they laughed at her because she didn't know what place the Yankees were in, or who the conductor of the Philharmonic was. To them she was just a humorless middle-aged woman who never seemed to relax. Well, they were right; but they were also mostly her subordinates. If they wanted to go to the opera or muse about aliens that was their business. Her business was catching criminals.

For the most part. What law had Tenon broken? Some immigration statute? She smiled to herself. There! Wasn't that humor?

She walked around the perimeter of the compound. He would have to have scaled the fence to get out, she noted. She couldn't have done it, but it wasn't impossible, especially on a clear night, with the guards facing the other way, with your life at stake. The man—the alien—must have wanted desperately to get away, for him to venture out into a strange planet unaided. And who would want to aid him? Someone who took pity on him for the danger he was in? Or was there something more going on here, some dark plot, the revelation of which would astonish everyone?

Doubtful. She could but hope.

She kicked at the snow, hoping to spot a torn swatch of alien cloth, a few drops of alien blood. If there had been any footprints, they were gone now, as soldiers had tramped back and forth across the snow in the search. Well, she would find nothing in the dark.

A piercing wind sprang up and made her shiver. Best to go in and get some rest, she thought. It would be a long day tomorrow. She retraced her steps to the motel.

She was beginning to feel that nothing would come easy in this case. Sometimes you get a sense of the way the criminal's mind is working, and everything just falls into place. Not this time, though. How would she figure out what was in an alien's mind? For that matter, did they have minds?

She sighed and walked into the lobby, vaguely aware of the stares directed at her. *The woman from the FBI. The one that's going to hook us up to the lie detectors.* She was used to that sort of thing. She went up to her room and took a hot bath.

Then she went to bed and dreamed, not of aliens but of needles, quivering wildly and then stopping to point, inexorably, at the guilty person.

11

By 8:30 the interrogations were underway. Important people first—just a few minutes of your time, Professor, purely a formality—ushered into the second-floor motel rooms, run through a series of questions West had composed, then courteously thanked and excused.

Thus it wasn't until late in the morning that Jerry Coleman of the Boston FBI office reached Angela Summers. He had been in the business long enough to know that she was hiding something, even before he had strapped the sensors to her. There was a different quality to the nervousness, intangible but readily apparent to him. Too bad: she seemed like a nice lady. When he had finished the questions he asked her to wait where she was for a few moments. She looked as if she had expected that. He went to find Madeleine West.

"She's an interpreter?" West asked, trying to keep the surprise and irritation out of her voice. It didn't pay to show your emotions. This was hard, though, very hard.

"Yeah, I gather they have about half a dozen of them who've learned the language. They're sort of the go-betweens in all the conversations."

"I see." Was she getting old, she wondered. Why hadn't she realized there had to be interpreters? Her lack of interest in the aliens was no excuse for not having thought the matter through. The aliens would need interpreters; only interpreters could be suspects, because only they could communicate with an alien crew member. Damn. She took it one step further, called Bacquier, and found out which interpreter had accompanied him to see Zanla the previous evening. Well, at least her stupidity hadn't cost them too

79

much time; and no one else had seen the obvious, either.

"May I see her dossier, please?"

Coleman slid it across the table to her.

West studied it: *summa cum laude . . . Ph.D. . . . twenty-seven languages* (Jesus!) *. . . associate professor . . . registered Democrat . . . practicing Catholic . . .* She picked up the phone and talked to Bacquier again. This was turning out to be fairly interesting after all.

Angela Summers sat in the motel room, alone except for the machine that had been her undoing. She had been terribly apprehensive before, but now that they knew about her, now that her life was about to come crashing down around her, she felt strangely serene. Following your conscience was ultimately liberating, she reflected. No one can really hurt you if you are willing to accept the consequences.

After a long while the man who had operated the polygraph returned. He brought a woman with him. She was middle-aged, a trifle overweight but healthy-looking. Her short black hair was liberally flecked with gray. There were deep lines around her eyes. She wore no makeup. She looked like a woman who was used to giving orders. She did not make Angela feel very comfortable.

"My name is West," the woman said.

"How do you do," Angela replied.

The woman nodded and sat down. "Well," she said, "our machine says you've been lying to us. Would you care to tell us the truth?"

Angela said nothing.

West tapped a manila folder with her index finger. "You're in a lot of trouble," she said. "Don't make things worse for yourself by not cooperating."

"If I'm in trouble I should get a lawyer," Angela observed.

West ignored her. "You're a religious person. How can you justify lying?"

You do not understand religion, Angela thought. But she was right, it was not pleasant to lie, even in a worthy cause. She considered carefully, and told the truth. Some of it. "I met Tenon and spoke with him," she said. "I admit that. But I did not help him escape. I did not know he wanted to escape. I do not know where he is now. And I won't say anything more without a lawyer."

"You talked with him about religion?"

Angela stared at her and said nothing. She stifled an urge to smile. She was in trouble, yes, but it wasn't the end of the world. And Tenon was free. They couldn't find him; they were worried. It was part of the pattern, of course: not what she had expected or hoped would happen, but what did that matter? She hoped Tenon had found some friends. She would pray for him.

West stood up abruptly, slapping the folder against her thigh. "Thank you for your time, Ms. Summers. You are free to go. But you will not be allowed to leave the compound." She nodded coldly to Angela and left the room.

West was nettled, but not surprised or discouraged. Interrogation of a woman like that would be difficult and probably fruitless at this point. And it was not impossible that she was telling her the truth. The sequence of events made sense: Tenon talks with her, finds out about religious freedom, decides to flee the ship on his own. But if he were still alive then someone, wittingly or unwittingly, had to have helped him. There was not much she could do if the assistance had been unwitting—a truckdriver picking up a confused-looking foreigner wandering along the highway, and then forgetting about it, for example. That was pretty farfetched, though. More likely someone knew who Tenon was, and was holding on to him for his own reasons.

But what could they be? She sighed, and studied Angela's folder some more. After she had finished with it she went to see Bacquier.

"Are you making progress?" he inquired hopefully. "It is hard to believe Ms. Summers had anything to do with this."

"Well, she is our best lead at the moment. Tell me, has she been allowed to go to Mass frequently since she came here?"

"Every day. With an escort. She just goes to church and comes back."

"But conceivably she could talk to people inside the church."

"I suppose so. I don't know whether the soldier goes inside with her or not. Who do you imagine she would speak to? I just can't see—"

"Neither can I. However, it's what we have so far. I'm going to talk to the pastor."

"Very well. You're the specialist."

"Yes. And of course, don't let her out of the compound for any reason until this thing is cleared up."

Bacquier nodded. "Of course."

Father Gardner was paying bills when the doorbell rang. He considered not answering, but that was foolishness; it was the middle of the day. Aliens came only in the dead of night. And besides, he hated paying bills.

The woman at the door was pleasant and efficient-looking—like a nurse, he thought, or an executive secretary. "Good afternoon, Father. I wonder if I might talk with you for a few moments?"

She was holding something out to him. It took a moment for him to focus on it, and another moment to comprehend. He felt himself flush. He knew she was watching him, observing his reactions, but there was nothing he could do. His flush only deepened. "Of course, Ms.—?"

"West."

"Won't you come in?"

He brought her into his office. She sat where Angela Summers had sat. Could he be arrested?

"Father, I want to ask you some questions about an interpreter from the Alien Study Team by the name of Angela Summers. Are you acquainted with her?"

How much did they know? Was this woman just toying with him? Never in his life had he wanted so much to lie—no, not lie, to run away and hide. He was a child again, desperate to escape his parents' wrath. But it was too late. "She—uh, I believe she attends Mass here at Most Precious Blood."

"Have you seen her speaking with anyone while she was in church?"

He shrugged helplessly. "I don't know what you mean. She sits by herself, I believe."

"Before or after Mass—any contact with anyone?"

"I—I don't think so. I can't be sure, of course. It could have happened."

"Have you spoken with her?"

She was just leading up to that, of course. Wanted to see the priest squirm. Well, if she knew, then what was the sense of squirming? He would just tell the truth. They couldn't find Bernardi—at least not through him. And they couldn't put him in jail for what he had done. At least, he didn't think so. "Yes," he replied firmly.

"Do you have any opinion of her?"

"She seems like a fine, religious woman. I admire her."

The FBI agent was silent for a moment, then abruptly stood up. "Well, thank you for your time, Father. If I have any more questions I'll let you know."

"Yes, uh, certainly." He saw her to the door and stared after her as she walked away. Had he missed something? Had he unconsciously given her some vital clue? He felt vaguely let down. Moments of courage were not frequent for him. Something at least should *happen* when one occurs. He sighed and went back to his bills. Something would happen eventually, he was quite certain.

Madeleine West sat in her official car and tried to puzzle it out. Something about that man had been unsettling. He had been quite clearly uncomfortable, which was not surprising, but there had been something more, something out of place. Fear, perhaps? Well, she had the resources. She might as well use them. She took her phone out of her pocket and dialed a number. "This is Madeleine West," she said into the receiver. "I'd like some background on Father Gardner, pastor of Most Precious Blood Catholic Church in Greenough. Whatever you can dig up on short notice: interviews with neighbors, school records, log of recent phone calls, any suspicious activities. You know the stuff. Keep it cool, though." There, that would keep a couple of rookies busy for a while.

It was late in the afternoon when a rookie interrupted her dossier-reading with some information he thought might be of interest to her. A few minutes later she drove back to the rectory, and had a long, serious talk with Father Gardner. Then she went back to the compound and called her boss.

Things were getting a bit *too* interesting now.

12

Ed Fitzgerald enjoyed meeting with the President, most of the time. Most of the time his people did their jobs properly, and that meant the President would be pleased. The President liked competence.

By rights the meeting he was on his way to should have been particularly enjoyable, therefore. His agent had cracked the case inside a day; well, at least she was started on cracking it. Pretty impressive, anyway. But Fitzgerald was nothing if not an astute judge of character, and he had a feeling the President would not be pleased. Not with what he had to tell him.

The White House was virtually deserted this time of night, the tourists long gone, the secretaries out partying with congressional staffers, the hotshot aides all home in bed dreaming of ways to speed up their careers. Fitzgerald had been a hotshot once himself. The rooms he passed were dim and silent, the corridors empty. Only important events happened here at midnight. Well, this would be no exception.

Jim Elias met him outside the Oval Office. He was dressed in suede pants and a silk shirt. God help us: was that the fashion nowadays? "Better be good," Elias said as they shook hands. "I was in the middle of a heavy date."

"You're not old enough to go on a date by yourself, are you?" Fitzgerald asked.

Elias shook his head. "I'm really not, but I got a friend at the FBI to forge me an ID so I could buy beer."

"They do good work over there, I hear. Is himself in?"

"After me."

Harold Gibson was striding toward them, hand outstretched, as they entered the room. He didn't look like a

85

man who had been up since five that morning. Fitzgerald dreaded Gibson's handshake. He always ached for hours afterward. "Mr. President."

"Fitzie, good to see you. Have a drink?"

"Oh well, if you insist."

Gibson smiled and gestured to Elias, who was already getting out the Jameson's. The kid dressed funny, but his memory was amazing.

"Sit sit sit. Don't tell me, you have good news. The alien's back in the ship, the Numoi are happy, God's in His Heaven, all's right with the world."

Fitzgerald sat and sipped his Jameson's. "Well, not exactly. God does enter into this, though."

"You intrigue me. Tell us everything, from the very beginning. You have thirty seconds."

Fitzgerald took a somewhat larger sip. Gibson sat opposite him, his eyes boring into Fitzgerald's skull, trying, so it seemed, to suck all the useful information out of him so that he wouldn't have to be bothered with a time-wasting conversation. The President could be quite intimidating if you weren't used to him.

"Here's what we have, as best we can figure it. This alien—his name is Tenon—secretly belongs to some forbidden religious cult on Numos. He had a conversation with one of the UN interpreters a couple of days ago, and evidently something came up about religious freedom here. So the fellow jumped ship and made his way into town, where he met up with the local parish priest. This priest handed him over to a friend of his, another priest, and the two of them took off. We have our best people tracking them down right now. Is my time up?"

Gibson's eyes shifted momentarily, puzzling it out. "Doesn't make sense," he said. "Why would the priests help this guy?"

"That's not entirely clear to me. There seem to be some correspondences between his beliefs and Christianity. Also, presumably he would be put to death if he gets sent back to his ship."

The President shook his head. "Still sounds funny." Then he paused. "You've got something more. What is it?"

Very astute. And now the sticky part. "The way we

broke this," Fitzgerald said, "was by getting the log of this parish priest's long-distance calls. On the night of Tenon's disappearance there was an overseas call placed. To the Vatican. To a personal number assigned to the Pope's private secretary. This local priest says his pal—name of Bernardi—won't let go of Tenon without Clement's say-so. The Vatican is evidently in this thing up to their scapulars."

"Good grief. This private secretary—what's his name?"

"Collingwood. He's an American."

Gibson turned to Elias, who was slouched in a chair across the room.

"He's in his late thirties," Elias said, "ambitious, intelligent, kind of a cold fish. I thought he was still in America, at the synod or whatever you call it in New York City."

"Would he get involved in something like this without the Pope's knowledge?"

"Doubt it. He knows who controls his future. He's a team player."

The President was silent. Fitzgerald braced himself. It was about time for Gibson to get angry. "Goddammit," he roared on schedule. "What kind of Mickey Mouse shit are those assholes trying to pull? I've put my head on the block for them! I've kept them in business in this country! If they tried they couldn't come up with anything that could be more damaging to me. I've got half of Congress screaming for blood because I've handed the aliens over to the UN— as if the aliens were some sort of goddam national treasure—and now the Vatican has set one of them loose on the countryside." His eyes riveted on Fitzgerald. "And you're doing a fine job of keeping it secret, by the way. The *Post* and the *Times* have already all but said flat out that it's an alien we're after."

Fitzgerald's ears hurt. He was getting a headache. "You can't do an investigation like this in total secrecy," he offered. "Not and get any results."

"Fat lot of results we've gotten," Gibson muttered, but it was clear that his anger had spent itself. Elias looked bored. This must happen every half-hour during the day. If only he weren't so *loud*. After a moment the President smiled and said, "Now let's get constructive. What is our response?"

"Finding the alien would help," Elias remarked.

Fitzgerald shrugged. "We've got our best people on it." Nice little phrase. No arguing with *that*.

"You know," Elias went on, "Clement is not the world's number-one ace political strategist. It may be that he's just acting reflexively here. This guy lands in the Church's lap asking for sanctuary, and they grant it. They don't consider anything else."

"So where does that leave us?"

"Well, we bring other considerations to his attention. Tell him the alien isn't worth his tax-exempt status in America. And so on. Put the screws to him. Diplomatically, of course."

Gibson nodded thoughtfully and turned to Fitzgerald. "You a Catholic, Fitzie?"

He spread his palms. "You know how it is."

Gibson sighed. "I have difficulty dealing with religious people. They look at everything so differently, you know?"

"Like Republicans," Fitzgerald suggested.

The President laughed—loud enough to wake Lincoln's ghost, Fitzgerald thought. "What time is it in Italy?" Gibson asked Elias.

"Seven A.M.," he answered promptly.

"Jesus, what a mind. Offhand, would you happen to know the Pope's phone number?"

13

The Pope's office was bare and functional—far from the baroque opulence of some of his predecessors, far even from the sleek modernism of a Paul. The walls held nothing but a cheap crucifix and portraits of Pious the Tenth and John the Twenty-third. The only artworks worth mentioning were a couple of ancient sculptures rescued from the Vatican grottoes.

Clement was well aware that people admired the simplicity of his life. "Whatever else you might say about him," he could imagine them remark, "he certainly doesn't pamper himself." It was an odd quirk of fate, he felt, that the things people praised him for he found totally unworthy of praise. He could not help being uninterested in material possessions; that was the way he was. May as well praise an Irishman for having red hair, or a German for being able to speak German. If someone had placed a Della Robbia in front of his desk, he would not have noticed it; if the most expensive wine in the world had been served for his dinner, it would not have tempted him.

In some people, of course, such abstinence *would* have been a virtue. While his celibacy, for example, had been no intolerable burden, he knew of many priests whose struggle to maintain *theirs* had been truly heroic. For some people, just living from day to day was a triumph of the will.

Ah yes, his humility too was well known. Always deprecating himself; his virtues are worthless, his vices numberless. Clement was aware that his protestations could sound ludicrous.

That was the trouble, of course. He was aware of so much, and so incapable of doing anything about it.

He sat in his chair (a special orthopedic chair, one creature comfort he was almost forced to allow himself) and consulted his schedule for the day. Nine o'clock meeting with Cardinal DiStefano to discuss reorganization of the Congregation of the Faith. Eleven o'clock audience in the Hall of the Consistory. Twelve o'clock audience with the South American ambassadors . . . He shoved the paper aside. It was easy to fill up the days just being a symbol. At least he was not a disgrace to his office. God had seen fit not to make him totally incapable.

The knock sounded lightly on the door, and Collingwood's face appeared immediately afterward. "You wanted to see me, Holiness?"

"Come in, Anthony. Sit."

Collingwood sat on the other side of the desk. No trace of worry or deception. He had once thought himself good at spotting such things. He was no longer very sure of his skill. "Anthony, I want you to tell me about the phone call you received from America two nights ago."

Collingwood was silent for a moment. The confrontation didn't seem to trouble him. "It was Father Bernardi," he replied. "The alien had escaped from his ship, and Bernardi wanted to know what to do with him. We agreed he should go into hiding with Tenon until you told him otherwise."

Clement fingered his pectoral cross. "And why, Anthony, did we learn of this from the President of the United States, and not from you?"

That cracked Collingwood's composure a bit. He pushed at his glasses and rubbed his nose. "I'm sorry," he said finally. "That must have been unpleasant for you. I felt I should wait, you see—"

"Because if the alien were caught before you told me then you would not have been implicated in this harebrained scheme?"

"It is not a scheme, Holiness," Collingwood protested. "If the alien had been handed over to the UN he would have been sent back to the ship. It would have been like turning a Jew over to the Nazis—or a Christian over to Nero. We just wanted to save his life."

Collingwood had made that point about the Jews before.

Clever fellow: you don't want to be another Pious the Twelfth, do you? "You have taken quite a risk, Anthony," Clement remarked. "You have put us in a very delicate, a very painful position without our knowledge or approval. I would be perfectly justified in dismissing you, in ending your career in the Church. It would save face with the President, it would show I can be a forceful leader. Why shouldn't I do this?"

The priest shrugged and said nothing.

Clement's back had begun to hurt. He stood up and walked over to the window. At this early hour only the pigeons and a few hardy tourists inhabited the vast expanse of Saint Peter's Square. He had seen it full of waving, cheering people, jumping up and down to get a glimpse of *him*. "Gibson said: 'I've put my head on the block for your Church. You can't expect me to keep it there, if this is what you pull.' A blunt man, the President."

"What is he going to do?"

"He has given us until one o'clock our time to put in motion steps for the return of Tenon. If we haven't done so by then, he will let it be known that he has switched positions on the tax-exemption bill."

"And what are you going to do?"

Clement sighed. His father always asked him that: what are you going to do? What are your plans? You must always be aiming for something, always have something in mind. Do your best, get ahead. "Did I ever tell you about the moment when I decided to become a priest?"

"No, your Holiness."

A little surprised, perhaps? Wondering if the old man's mind was starting to wander? "It was during the Blitz. World War II, you know. A bomb hit our house. A beam fell on my father and me. My father died instantly. I wasn't injured badly, although my back hasn't been right since. But I was trapped, under the beam, with my dead father. It was only for a few minutes, though it seemed like an eternity. It was long enough to decide my life.

"For all he was a devout Catholic, my father had a kind of Protestant outlook on life. He believed that hard work was virtue, that if one did one's duty and made one's plans, then one would be rewarded. He was right, he was a moderately successful shopkeeper, widely respected, a pillar of the Church, had a son who never gave him any trouble. And then his house fell on top of him and crushed him to death.

"This of course is the situation that turns most people into bitter atheists. God works in mysterious ways. I was twelve at the time, and not aware of the appropriate reaction. To me, hurt and scared and sad, what had happened meant this: the things of this world are of no importance. Your home, your possessions, your very life can be of little value if they exist at the whim of a crazy German who needs living space. If anything matters, it must be what is beyond life. My father's body was a broken toy, but his soul was with God. I knew at that instant that I could only tolerate this life if I devoted my own to what lay beyond it.

"Well, you may wonder what this has to do with Gibson's threat."

"I presume it means you will not give in to it," Collingwood said.

Clement smiled. "Am I that transparent?"

"Your decision is nevertheless surprising," Collingwood noted. "What we believe at age twelve is not always what makes us act at age seventy-two."

"Yes, you are quite right. When I was beneath that beam I did not have every church and monastery and parochial school in America to worry about. Just my own fatherless future. No matter. What are the chances of Bernardi being found?"

"In the short run, slim, I would say. Bernardi is no one's fool. Ultimately they are bound to catch him, I suppose. But the alien ship is supposed to be leaving soon. If Bernardi can hold out until the ship goes, then Tenon's chances of survival are presumably pretty good. Of course, all of this seems to rule out putting pressure on the Numoi to change their ways, but it doesn't—"

"Yes. We will need to tell the world, to justify what we are doing. If Gibson wishes to reverse his stand on the tax bill, we must make clear that he is doing so out of pique at us, because we are trying to keep him from sending an innocent person to death for his religious beliefs. We must show that extraordinary events demand extraordinary responses, even from such a conservative Church as ours."

"This is quite exciting, Holiness. I—"

"Yes, well. We live in exciting times. Can you write me a statement?"

"By one o'clock our time?"

"Better make it noon. There are a few cardinals who will have to see it first, and they will then have to be given artificial respiration."

"Of course. And my—uh—indiscretion?"

Clement shugged. "You should have told me. You know that. Tell me from now on. There are few enough people I can trust in this world, Anthony. I would like you to be one of them."

"Yes, your Holiness." Collingwood looked appropriately chastened. He knelt and kissed Clement's ring before departing.

Clement sat back down. He felt nervous but strangely happy, now that the first impulsive step had been taken. He was certain that he could face down Fontanelli and the rest of the cardinals. They could fuss and fume and threaten, but ultimately a Pope is beyond anyone's threats, if he chooses to be.

And why had he chosen this issue on which to be unyielding? The Holy Spirit, the mystical part of him was inclined to say, the rational part countered: this is just too clear-cut. One cannot send a person to his death in exchange for a tax break.

Clement tried to imagine himself as a hunted man on an alien planet: friends, culture, everything gone. All that remained was the fact of your existence, and that was tenuous at best. What keeps you alive? What was the purpose of running, if there is nothing to run to?

It was not so different, he reflected, from lying in darkness, a beam across your back, in the midst of pain and death. To survive in either case you had to decide that what mattered was you and the infinite, not you and your friends, or you and your world. And your existence matters only in that it gives glory to God.

Yes. Tenon had risked martyrdom, after his own lights,

had given up everything for the glory of God. In the abstract, Clement knew he could do the same, but only once in his life had he been called upon to prove it. Well, good for Tenon then. He was young. He knew what he believed in, and he acted on it.

Also, he had been very lucky so far. Good—then Clement would be a part of his luck. He glanced at his schedule. Should he tell them now, or wait for Anthony's statement? The Congregation of the Faith could come later, if necessary. But no, he would get the statement first. Best to know exactly how he was going to throw the Church into an uproar, before he actually did it.

14

Claude Bacquier glared at his secretary as she tiptoed meekly in and laid the statement on the desk in front of him. She was afraid of him, he knew, and with good reason. Diplomats need not be diplomatic with their secretaries. A lot of pressure built up in his job; he had to get rid of it somehow. If he suffered, his staff suffered too.

He managed to keep from snapping at her for being so slow in getting the damn thing, but he couldn't bring himself to thank her for it. So he just tried to ignore her while she beat her retreat. Then he adjusted his cuffs, picked it up, sighed, and read.

He already knew what was in it; he just wanted to see it in print, to confirm its reality.

". . . . We have been made aware of the existence of a certain religion on the home planet of the Numoi. . . . While we do not advocate interfering in the internal affairs of the Numoi (even if that were possible), we do feel that the study of this religion should be made the highest priority in the humans' dealings with this race. And we feel, further, that it should be made clear to the Numoi that the people of Earth hope and pray that the existence of this religion will not be threatened. . . ."

And what the hell is that but interfering in their internal affairs, you stupid old goat, Bacquier muttered inwardly. He found the use of the pontifical *we* particularly irritating. Who are *we*? You and God? You and the half-billion people who don't go to church, don't remember any of your dogma, and don't agree with half your opinions, but who call themselves Catholics because they had some water poured over them when they were too young to object?

95

People like me, Bacquier realized. Speak for yourself, Clement.

". . . We are protecting this person because he has asked us for sanctuary, and because to return him to his masters would be to condemn him to certain death. We are fully aware of the consequences of our action, both for the Church and for relations between Earth and the Numoi. We feel, however . . ."

Fully aware. *Merde.* Bacquier thought of all he and Aronson had accomplished in the past few months: building the compound, getting the interpreters to work, negotiating the information exchange, choosing the scientists, arranging the system, keeping everyone happy, working toward a stable and mutually beneficial relationship where all the doomsayers had predicted interplanetary holocaust. His Holiness was fully aware he might be causing some little problems. His Holiness was blithely ruining the greatest triumph of Claude Bacquier's career. His Holiness could go—

"What is it?" he barked in response to his secretary's buzz.

"The Secretary-General, sir. On twelve."

Bacquier took a deep breath and picked up the phone. "Bacquier here."

"Ah, Claude, this is most distressing, is it not?"

Ashanti's voice betrayed no hint of distress. Neither would his. "It certainly complicates matters, sir."

"President Gibson was just speaking with me. He seemed quite distraught."

Noted. "He would have every reason to be."

"And so would you, Claude. Certainly you have the most difficult task of all: explaining the situation to Zanla."

Again, noted. "Would you have any suggestions as to how this task might be carried out?"

"Well, certainly it should be done immediately. Emphasis should be placed on the largeness of our planet, the swiftness of our transportation systems, the degree of similarity of the Numoi's appearance to ours, the lack of control we have over the Pope. Point out the diligence of our search, the help that this new information has given us.

Hint very carefully that this situation is due in part to his own carelessness in supervising his crew members."

"I take it, then, that if Tenon is found he will still be returned to the Numoi, despite the public knowledge that he will be put to death."

"That is our present intention. You may also, however, obtain assurances from Zanla that Tenon will not be harmed."

"What if he refuses to give such assurances?"

Bacquier could visualize Ashanti's thin, enigmatic smile. "What he says is not what matters. What we report that he says is what matters. Is that not true, Claude?"

"Quite true. I will speak to him immediately. A statement should be available for the evening news."

"Excellent."

Bacquier hung up. He always found conversations with Ashanti quite satisfying. Everything was calm and clear and ordered. Everything was in perspective. He stood up and buttoned his suit coat. He would apologize to his secretary, and then see Zanla.

Paul Aronson waylaid Bacquier in the lobby. "What are we going to do?" he asked.

Bacquier shrugged. "Tell Zanla what's happening. Keep looking. I just spoke with Ashanti."

"Did he mention anything about changing his mind—about keeping Tenon when we find him?"

Bacquier shook his head. "It's no good, Paul. You know we can't do that."

"An hour's interview—that might be enough. Look, Ashanti might not even have to know."

"I understand how you are feeling, Paul," Bacquier responded in his best diplomatic style. "But you know I can't do that. The policy is set. Please understand." He squeezed Aronson's arm and hurried off.

Aronson gazed after him. No, you do not understand, he thought, and he trudged back to his office. Stacks of reports and meetings summaries cluttered his desk, but he knew he wouldn't be able to concentrate on them. His staff had given him a paperweight for Christmas—a sparkling blue pyramid. He picked it up and hefted it in his hand, wondering if he would get any satisfaction from pitching it through his window. Not enough, he decided. He sat down and sulked.

His job had its highs and lows, and right now he was in one of the lows. A distressing sequence of events had been playing itself out in his mind more and more frequently lately: the Numoi leave, with their secret of faster-than-light travel still intact. The years go by, the Numoi never return, and scientists batter their heads—no, he batters *his* head—against the unyielding problem. And what good would all the facts about Numian zoology and geology and sociology be, without an understanding of this one difference that set them above and apart from humans?

Damn diplomats. Just an hour with the guy, to ask a few questions that might revolutionize our understanding of the universe. Was that being a pig-headed scientist?

Damn. He threw the paperweight toward a metal wastebasket across the room. It went in with a resounding bang that made his eardrums throb. That helped some.

Not enough.

Ergentil had wanted to sit in on this latest meeting, but Zanla had forbidden it. That was his right. He had not been nasty about it, however, and had promised to talk it all out with her afterward. Was it possible that he was preparing himself, slowly, for the disagreeable task of admitting she was right? Not very likely.

The problem between them was personal, of course, but also doctrinal, and that was what worried Ergentil the most. The Ancients had always been at their fuzziest in describing the purpose of these journeys through space. To teach us humility, Gontor had said, by bringing us into closer contact with all-that-is. Lesser writers had said that humility would be taught by meeting creatures of other races, but generations of crews unreturned and crews returning with the same stories of blackness and void had made these predictions suspect. There was still support, though, for the theory that their ultimate goal was the discovery of rational alien life. And that was what Zanla had seized on in formulating his policy toward the aliens: what is the good of just seeing this life, he had argued, without communicating with it, without learning from it?

Hard to disagree with in the abstract. But Ergentil had quickly seen where it was heading in reality: toward a mindless lust for the aliens' awesome machines and weapons. How had we managed to live for so long without being able to speak with someone on the other side of the planet at the pushing of a button? Why have we never invented these marvelous devices that explode on signal and kill thousands of one's enemy?

And this, Ergentil knew, was wrong. It verged on heresy, like that of the old cult, never entirely suppressed, that insisted on worshiping the Ship, despite the clear pronouncements of the Ancients that the Ship was the means and not the goal. These alien machines would quickly and utterly destroy the delicate balance between life and thing that had been the great achievement of her civilization. Already people grew complacent, ignored the old ways, forgot the meaning and greatness of what had been accomplished: look at how this new religion attracted them. They were ripe for conquest, intellectually as well as physically. These meetings with the aliens were simply preparing the way.

She knew, of course, that people considered priestesses to be a sour, dreary lot, always calling down the wrath of the Ancients on the decadent modern ways. They much preferred the more dashing, pragmatic Masters. But it had always been that way. She had her beliefs and she would fight for them; she had her job, and she would do it.

There was a knock on her door. "Enter," Ergentil said glumly. It was Zanla, looking ill at ease in enemy territory. She motioned to a chair, and he sat down in silence.

"It does not appear that Tenon has been returned to us," Ergentil noted.

"Your conclusion is correct."

"What did this Bacquier tell you—or is that no business of a priestess?"

"I didn't come here to talk over repairs to the waste-disposal system with you."

Ergentil made an ironic half-bow. "Then?"

"Tenon is in the hands of a religious group that has beliefs similar to the followers of Chitlan, according to Bacquier. They are demanding that Earth make tolerance for these Chitlanians a precondition for further development of relations between them and us."

"But that is absurd," Ergentil exploded. "How dare they?"

Zanla spread his hands in a gesture of ignorance. "Tenon evidently heard of them through one of the interpreters, escaped, and sought sanctuary with them. They are now keeping him in hiding. This group is evidently large and well organized and legal. Bacquier says—"

"Bacquier says, Bacquier says. How do you know that anything he says is the truth?"

"I don't, of course. He could be holding Tenon himself, and have found out all this about Chitlan directly from him. The story does have a surface plausibility, though."

"Well, what do you suggest we do then? Wait around here as long as his story remains plausible? Let the Council inscribe our names in the Square of the Ancients, let the aliens perfect their transportation and weapons and follow us home?"

"It is my feeling," Zanla responded slowly, "that we must make some positive effort to get Tenon back. I agree we should not sit here idly and let events take their course, but I also think that leaving Tenon behind is dangerous to the security of Numos."

"Then what do you propose?"

Zanla was silent. Ergentil threw her arms up in disgust. "Nothing. You have nothing."

"If I do not have a plan by midday tomorrow, we will leave without Tenon."

"And if your plan does not work?"

"If I have a plan, it will work."

They stared at each other. Of what value was the dignity of her position, Ergentil thought (hardly for the first time), if ultimately she had no authority in a situation like this? Zanla was the Master. He had the power to play out his game to the bitter end. She motioned him out of her room. At least she had power here.

He stood up. "I know you do not agree, but—"

"It has gone too far," she interrupted wearily. "No matter what the outcome, Numos is in peril. Let that be your burden, Master."

He bowed stiffly and left.

Vomurd, she thought. Playing out a game whose outcome is predetermined. Was it predetermined that her world would collapse, that the Chitlanians would take over her temples, that these soulless aliens would sit in the Council Palace? What a cruel trick for existence to play!

She recalled the first Departure she had ever witnessed: her initial year at the temple school, fresh from the countryside, shy, in awe of everything, but especially the Ship. The previous one had not returned, so this was a gleaming, brand-new creation, standing proudly in the triangular *golossi*, awaiting the brave crew that would give meaning to its existence.

The monitors had roused them in the chilly predawn and herded them through the gray streets to their place of honor not far from the stairway. "Remember," Marsta had whispered to them, "if you are good girls and learn your lessons well, then someday you too may go on the Voyage."

The girls were all appropriately solemn, but none more so than Ergentil, as the crew, in their ceremonial tunics, filed slowly across the Square of the Ancients, across the stones inscribed with the names of those who had not returned, ignoring the huge crowd that surrounded them, eyes fixed on the glorious blue pyramid, proud of themselves, proud of their race.

And then they had gone inside, and Ergentil waited, hands clasped tight to the edge of the stone bench, as the sun rose and the shadow of the pyramid lengthened, lengthened, and she visualized the men and women, eyes closed, minds linked, ready to become part of all-that-is, willing it to happen. . . .

And the shadow hit the far edge of the square, and the gleaming blue Ship shimmered and disappeared, leaving behind a crowd that stirred and buzzed, and a girl whose soul longed to be with it.

So now you're here, she thought. Part of the dream. At odds with the Master, ignored by the crew, no longer sure of yourself or your religion. If the Ancients could have found a way to take that childish faith and make a pill out of it, they would have been far better off.

Still, the pattern had begun. There was nothing to be done but see it through. Masters went on several Voyages, Priestesses on only one. This was *her* Voyage; there would be no other.

15

"Jesus Christ, you shoulda been there," Fitzgerald said. "I've never seen him so p.o.'d. I thought the walls in the Oval Office would crack. You ever seen Gibson when he's in one of those fits?"

"No, sir," Madeleine West replied.

"I'll bet he had an even worse one when he heard what the Pope did. He was pretty calm by the time he got back to me, though."

"What did he say?"

"Well, full speed ahead, of course. He also wanted a progress report, which is why I called you, obviously. Got the guy yet?"

"Sorry."

"Can't win 'em all. What *have* you got?"

West took a deep breath, marshaled her facts, and began. "We interviewed Bernardi's fellow priests at the Jesuit residence. No one saw him leaving or returning that night. He took a tan '99 Plymouth Excelsior minicoupe; apparently none of his personal possessions are missing. The conclusion is that he didn't return there after getting Tenon. There's no way of knowing how much money he had, but it couldn't have been a great deal. We put the Plymouth into the police computer identisystem as a top priority for the East Coast and Midwest. At ten this morning it was discovered parked on a side street near Penn Station in New York. There was a parking ticket on it written at 2:07 the day before yesterday, so we may assume they were in the city at some time before that. We have so far been unable to trace anything of their movements between Greenough and New York, and I doubt that we'll be able to."

"What about after New York?"

"Nothing. They could have taken a train, a plane, rented a car, you name it. However, without much cash they couldn't get very far unless they used a credit card. We're checking on that now."

"Hard to believe this guy Bernardi'd be stupid enough to use a credit card. It'd be like sending us a map."

"I agree. But there might be someplace he wanted to get to, where he'd feel secure. He might be willing to let us know the city he was headed for, let's say, aware that he'd have a day or two's head start. After all, he couldn't keep driving that Plymouth."

"He might still be in the city, though."

"That, I think, is more probable. Bernardi was raised in New York. He has all kinds of relatives and friends there. My feeling is that he came home for help—transportation or lodging. We've just got to do some legwork and see if that's true."

"What's this guy's background, anyway? He seems like kind of an odd one."

West reached for the paper on the far side of her desk. "Born 1961, New York City. Attended local parochial schools and Fordham University—where he met Anthony Collingwood, by the way. After graduation, entered the Jesuit Order in 1983, studied—"

"Yeah, yeah. Very interesting. What's the real poop, though?"

"Well, he's an only child. Father died when he was young. Very likable, athletic, socially active growing up. Sort of a natural leader, evidently, and religious besides. Not extremely brilliant, but the kind who gets things done. Talking to a couple of the Jesuits, I got the impression that he's been rather a disappointment to them. They seemed to have hoped he'd revitalize the entire order or something. Instead he just does his job and makes friends—including some strange ones, like this Father Gardner in Greenough, who appears to be kind of a loser. Bernardi teaches English, Italian, and coaches track at an exclusive Jesuit prep school near Greenough. The students adore him."

"Streetwise, huh? Tough? Maybe bored?"

"Hard to say. He certainly didn't waste any time getting involved in this affair."

"I think you've got your hands full, Madeleine."

"We'll see."

"So what will you do now?"

"I'm going to head back to New York and run things from there. Not much left to work on here in Massachusetts."

"Good, I'll tell the President the investigation is on the move."

West smiled. "Incidentally, uh, are there any limitations on us because of the Pope's statement?"

"Not that anyone's told me. I guess we may take some heat, but the UN people are trying to take care of that. Did you hear Bacquier's statement?"

"No."

"He just talked to Zanla, says the Numoi have no intention of putting Tenon to death. It's all a misunderstanding and so forth."

"Is that true?"

"Beats me. Why don't we just pretend it's true and see if that doesn't help the cause. Keep me posted, okay?"

"Yes, sir."

West didn't like these controversial cases. They always got messy, she reflected on the flight back to New York. She liked good guys and bad guys. She liked witnesses who were eager to cooperate. She didn't like having to worry about what the President, or the Pope, thought about what she was doing.

She still recalled with anger and dismay the investigation of the space-shuttle explosion, in which the Antitechnology Crusade insisted they had sabotaged the craft, and the government insisted the explosion had been due to pilot error, and nobody seemed very interested in finding out what had really happened. Or the case of the Middle Eastern diplomat who had kidnaped the seventeen-year-old D.C. high school gymnast . . .

Well, no sense dredging those things up. No job is perfect. This case could have been worse. She would do much better trying to figure out the thought processes of Father Bernardi than worrying about when Gibson and Fitzgerald were going to put the clamps on her. She felt the plane descend toward LaGuardia, and attempted to think like an underachieving Italian priest.

"If they're in New York, it looks pretty tough," Agent Dewey said. "No one is saying anything. They're protecting one of their own. We've tapped his mother's phone, a few cousins and friends, we've got a couple of stakeouts, but if he lies low and isn't stupid . . ." Dewey shrugged.

"You've talked to the mother?" West asked.

Dewey nodded. "She doesn't know what to make of any of this. She's got the Pledge of Allegiance framed on the wall of her apartment. But she wouldn't talk. Could hardly expect her to."

"Still, it's important. Bernardi must be pretty close to her, only son and all. If he's going to be in trouble, he might call, give her some information. Also, she'd be the one most likely to be able to run down all his friends."

"She didn't talk," Dewey repeated.

"I think I'll go have a chat with her myself."

Dewey made a you're-the-boss gesture. West didn't have time to worry about hurt feelings.

The apartment was nicer than West had anticipated. It was a co-op up near Columbia, complete with landscaping and security guards. A couple of lurking reporters waylaid her as she went in, but she brushed them aside. She didn't care much for reporters.

Mrs. Bernardi studied West's credentials for a long moment before letting her in. "There have been so many people," she said wearily.

She was a slight woman, in her late sixties, West guessed, with tinted hair and sharp features. She was wearing red slacks, a ruffled shirt, and open-toed sandals. West would not have supposed her to be Bernardi's mother.

The furnishings of the apartment also didn't go with her: chock full of Sacred Hearts, crucifixes, Infants of Prague, Virgin Marys, and other Catholic personages West couldn't identify. And, of course, pictures of her son: high school graduation, college graduation, ordination, Bernardi playing basketball, Bernardi toothless in the fourth grade. Tough to tell exactly who was being worshiped here. West noted a framed portrait of Pope Clement in the middle of one particularly crowded wall.

"Do you mind if I smoke?" Mrs. Bernardi asked. "I don't usually, but this business has got me so nervous."

"Not at all. Please do." West loathed the habit.

"I don't really know why you people have come back. I mean, I told that gentleman this morning that I don't know anything."

"You must understand we have to be persistent," West said with her winningest smile. "Perhaps you've thought of something in the meantime—some friend your son mentioned he might go to in a time of trouble, somebody who owed him a big favor."

Mrs. Bernardi took a deep drag. "Oh, everybody owed Albert favors. He's that kind of person. But you see, I don't understand why you'd think I would want to help you. I mean—he's my son. My only son. And you want to capture him."

"I can sympathize, Mrs. Bernardi. I have a son too," West lied. "And I wouldn't want any harm to come to *him*. But here's how I see it: the United States Government is committed to finding your son. No matter how many friends he has, sooner or later he will be caught. Now I don't know what will happen to him if he is caught. But I can assure you that things will be easier for him if he is found now than if he is found later after considerable damage has been done to our interests."

"But I can't see that he's committed any *crime*," Mrs. Bernardi exclaimed. "What law has he broken by going off with this poor unfortunate creature?"

"Well, I'm not a lawyer," West lied again, "so I couldn't say for sure. But—" West paused, looked uncertain, then asked: "Mrs. Bernardi, do you love your country?"

"Of course I do," Mrs. Bernardi replied defensively.

West nodded. "Good. I trust, then, that you will keep secret what I am about to tell you. I am breaking the law by even mentioning this. Mrs. Bernardi, your son is in grave danger."

The mother's eyes watered in an almost Pavlovian response. "Why?" she whispered.

West's eyes swept the room, as if looking for intruders or

microphones. "You must have heard that the aliens possess the secret of faster-than-light travel, something that Earth scientists have said is not even theoretically possible. Now it seems extremely likely that Tenon—the alien your son is protecting—has sufficient knowledge to give us the solution to this puzzle.

"At this very moment, Mrs. Bernardi, agents of foreign powers hostile to America are searching for your son. Do you realize what an advantage it would be to any nation to have this information? They could be masters of the world—perhaps of the Universe. And your son stands in their way. Do you think they will deal with him as fairly and justly as the United States Government would, Mrs. Bernardi?"

Mrs. Bernardi shook her head mutely. The ash on her cigarette, unheeded, dropped onto her slacks. She brushed at it hurriedly and then turned away from West, choking back a sob.

"Of course your son is a good man, a holy man," West continued. "He did what he thought was right. But we know now that no harm will come to this alien if he is returned to his ship. And we know that every moment the two of them are out there, unprotected, the danger for both of them increases. That's why it is so important that you tell us what you know."

West waited patiently while the woman cried. Finally the tears stopped and Mrs. Bernardi looked up at her. Behind the smeared makeup she looked terribly old. "I don't know anything," she whispered hoarsely. "Albert obeys the Pope. Tell the Pope he is in danger."

West sighed. "If that's how you feel, Mrs. Bernardi. We will have to do our best without your help. If anything should happen to . . . well. Thank you for your time."

"I don't know anything," Mrs. Bernardi repeated, her eyes pleading for understanding.

She was lighting another cigarette with trembling hands as West let herself out.

Back in the car West put on her phone. The message light was flashing. It was Dewey, asking her to call the office. At the next stoplight she obeyed.

"Any luck?" he asked her.

"Not yet. I'm pretty certain she knows something, though. She's close to cracking."

"Uh-huh. Of course, we may not need her."

West decided she didn't like Dewey. "Spill it," she commanded.

"A charge slip was just processed on Bernardi's Insta-credit card. Two one-way plane tickets to Las Vegas."

"Las Vegas," she repeated incredulously.

"You figure this alien's got a system to beat the slot machines?" Dewey asked.

West didn't bother to reply.

16

Zanla had not sought an insight since just after his student days, when his first Voyage had caused him to reconsider his entire life, to try to understand what made him the way he was.

Most people had no use for the exercise nowadays—couldn't see that it accomplished anything. Zanla hadn't even bothered to use it when they first arrrived on Earth, and he had had to make some tremendously important decisions. But now he needed it; and Elial, his teacher, who believed deeply in insights, had told him: when you feel you need it, that is when it will work.

He stood alone in the darkened Room of the Ancients, hands clasped behind his back, swaying slightly. A blue cape lay lightly on his shoulders, a rug was soft beneath his feet. He felt the pressure of the rug, the slight stretching of his arms, the weight of the cape. The search, as always, began inside.

He was alert but worried. Thinking too much with too little result. Thinking about the wrong things: about how this business would affect the stuttering progress of his career, about the difficult relationship between himself and Ergentil, about the memory that hung like a pall over all he tried to do. One by one he pushed these concerns out of his consciousness. They only got in the way of a pure consideration of the problem.

When they were gone he approached it, tentatively, timidly.

Tenon. Heretic, fool. Why hadn't he been discovered and weeded out? Zanla felt his anger swelling, but there was no insight in anger. If he were Tenon, then, what would he have done?

He tried, but the question was hopeless, and he quickly withdrew from it. It was more than he could do to pretend he was an enemy of Numos. Such creatures could only be despised.

A snatch of dialogue came into his mind. "Why do we explore the Universe?" he had asked Elial once, when he was a callow youth and thought he was capable of understanding such matters.

"To teach us humility," the Master had replied with a smile.

"But how can it teach us humility, if it only proves that we are the greatest beings in existence?"

"That you cannot understand until you have done it."

True. His arrogance had long been tempered by a perception of his race's insignificance in the scheme of all-that-is. When the *retheo* was set, the crew became powerless, at the mercy of chance and hostile darkness (if, of course, it had been set fairly, and not to one of the safe readings that guarantees a Master an uneventful Voyage and a mediocre career afterward). That sense of powerlessness, Elial had felt, was the central meaning of the Voyages.

Would Elial have felt the same about this first meeting with aliens? Had they searched for generations, in order to find a race that would tell them that all their achievements counted for nothing?

It was not impossible. Still, the one achievement remained—the one that had brought them here, the one that was now in danger. Humility need not imply abject surrender.

Purify the mind, then. What were the natives' weaknesses? How could he use his strength? Surely he had learned something in his time on this planet.

This planet. He thought of the first wary steps, hesitant breaths, he in front to show why he was fit for the Council, but fear clutching at him too.

He thought of the sky and the grass, the building and the wide black path that convinced him that here at last was a race that could build and—perhaps—think.

Walking slowly through the early-morning mist toward the building and the road, seeing the creature come out of the building and move in their direction, oblivious . . . knowing that the moment was at hand and wondering what the shifting patterns of fate would make of it for all of them.

Zanla saw the man's face see theirs, take in their short robes and silver chains, then notice the shining blue Ship overpowering the mist behind them. He saw the man back away slowly, then turn and run, hands in the air, shouting over and over a word that Zanla had since come to learn: "No! No! No!" The sound echoed in their minds as they waited uncertainly for the next shift in the patterns.

As ever, the insight came unbidden. This time it was as pure and enigmatic as Elial could have wished.

We are the creatures of their nightmares.

Zanla shifted his weight, and his mind moved as well, circling the thought, probing it, judging its truth. . . .

He could not tell. All he knew was that it gave him a plan, and before he had had no plan. It would not be perfect, but he doubted there was a better one.

He took off the blue cape, folded it carefully over his arm, and walked out of the room. Samish was waiting across the corridor. "Samish, how well can you speak the alien language?"

"A few words only, Master. Enough to communicate."

"You can't write it, I suppose."

"No, only the Priestess—"

"Yes, I know. Send her—no. I had better go to her myself."

An unavoidable consequence. She would either do it or not. He could only ask.

"Tell the human guards I want to see Bacquier at the morning session tomorrow. I will be with Ergentil now. We are not to be disturbed on any account."

She was, ultimately, persuaded, and early the next morning she brought him her work. He stared at it appraisingly, but it meant nothing to him. He had to trust her.

"Is it good enough?" he asked.

"I think so," she replied. "Good enough."

Zanla slipped the piece of paper into a small box behind his desk. "Thank you," he said. "Now we shall see."

* * *

Bacquier and the interpreter Natasha arrived promptly. They exchanged stiff bows and sat down. Zanla began immediately. "Do you have any good news for me?"

Bacquier shook his head as the interpreter relayed the question. "You must understand we are doing all we can," the answer came back. "Our governments are putting pressure on the Pope, and we are searching as thoroughly as possible. But it is a big planet, and the Pope refuses to help."

"Who is this Pope?"

"The leader of their religion."

"Can you not capture him and force him to give up Tenon?"

This seemed to make Bacquier uncomfortable. Good. The diplomat paused a couple of times in his reply. "It is not possible to do that, you see, Zanla. The Pope has many followers. He has no military power, but . . . to arrest or imprison him would create great problems. Besides, it is not likely he has specific knowledge of where Tenon is."

"But he could tell his followers to give him up, and they would obey, wouldn't they?"

"Yes, yes, I suppose so. But we cannot do more than we are doing. Please believe me."

Bacquier extended his hands slightly toward Zanla in a gesture that needed no interpretation. He seemed quite upset. Zanla found himself believing him. But that did not remove the need for action. The man was too worried about his internal problems, not enough about the power of the Numoi. It was time to change the balance.

"This is very serious, Claude," Zanla said. "We must return soon to Numos, but we cannot return without Tenon. I hope you can understand that. I hope you can understand that I do not want to do this. But I have no choice."

He stopped for Natasha to interpret and watched Bacquier's face. Nothing. He continued. "Tenon must be returned to us within three Earth-days. If he is not, this is what will happen: we will leave this place and reappear over an earth city. We will drop from the Ship papers that say: 'The governments of Earth must return our stolen crew member or this city will be destroyed.' We will do this over your major cities, all around your planet, as many of them as we can reach within two days. Then we will begin the process of destruction."

Bacquier remained impassive, but the shock and fear were unmistakable on the face of the interpreter. That was good. Bacquier uttered a sentence, his eyes fixed on Zanla. Natasha stumbled through it. "You cannot speak our languages, Zanla. How can you make people understand this message?"

Zanla reached behind him and removed the sheet of paper from the box. He slid it across the desk to Bacquier. "We are not your equals in learning languages, but we are not helpless, Claude. We have made use of the books you have given us."

Bacquier stared at the paper without picking it up. The interpreter too leaned over to read it. Yes, it was good enough, they understood it, it frightened them. Ergentil had done her job.

That point settled, Bacquier moved on, inevitably, to the next one. "All our information indicates that the Numoi are relatively primitive compared to our race in military capabilities, Zanla. I hope you will not be offended if I say that I do not believe you can carry out your threat."

"Certainly I am not. And likewise I hope you will not be offended if I say that what you believe does not matter. It does not even matter whether or not we can do it. What matters is what the rest of your race believes."

"What do you mean?" Bacquier asked, but it was clear he was beginning to understand.

"I mean the threat itself will be sufficient, even without weapons. People will stream out of your cities, trampling each other in their terror. Thieves and murderers will roam the streets, there will be riots, governments will be attacked, your economic and political systems will collapse. The people of your planet will demand that Tenon be returned."

Bacquier pondered. "The people can be warned beforehand," he observed. "Told it's all a bluff. Emergency plans can be prepared."

Zanla shook his head, human-style. "It will not work," he replied. "We are not talking about fires or floods or even human enemies. We are talking about *aliens*. Mysterious, powerful aliens. Creatures of your nightmares."

Bacquier shifted slightly in his chair when the interpreter reached the final phrase. Do diplomats have nightmares? Natasha's eyes were wide and worried. "This is a grave step you are taking, Zanla," Bacquier said finally. "You know that it will end the possibility of a peaceful development of relations between our worlds. And the point is, you still might not get Tenon back. If we cannot find him, we cannot find him."

"I repeat," Zanla replied, "I do not want to do this. But I will not back down. I must make it clear to all your governments that failure to return Tenon will do more than just anger me. It will produce suffering and chaos for your entire planet. Perhaps with that in mind you will not be so hesitant to capture this Pope and force him to reveal what he knows."

"Have you considered that this plan of yours is quite dangerous to you as well as to us?" Bacquier inquired slowly. "Few of our governments are likely to sit idly by while you carry out your threat. What good will come of this for any of us if your ship is destroyed?"

"If our ship is destroyed, your planet is destroyed," Zanla stated flatly. "Our weapons may not be as powerful as yours, but we have control of a physical process that is far beyond the comprehension of the greatest of your scientists. We have discovered the destructive power of this process before, to our dismay. You may tell this to your governments. They lose more by destroying us than by letting us carry out our threat."

Their eyes met in silence for a long moment. You do not believe me, Zanla thought. But can you take the risk? Can any of you? Of course not. Elial would not have approved of a lie. It was hardly fitting for one who wished to be a Councilor. But it was necessary. And it would work.

"I have no way of knowing if what you tell me is true," Bacquier said, breaking his gaze away from Zanla's. "If it is, then you are taking an even greater risk, and there is all the more reason why you shouldn't carry out your threat. Because I cannot guarantee that every nation—or any nation—will believe what you say. If you threaten to destroy them, they may just decide to drop a bomb on you and hope for the best. Do you want to be responsible for the destruction of what might be the only other intelligent race in the Universe?"

"I prefer to suppose that some member of this intelligent race will return Tenon to his masters, and all of us might return to our previous peaceful condition. Please keep me informed of any progress you make in the search."

Bacquier interpreted this correctly as his dismissal and rose from his chair. "I must beg you to reconsider, Zanla. There is too much at stake here to let your anger take hold of you this way."

"Please understand, Claude, it is not anger that is making me do this," Zanla replied truthfully. "I am only doing what has to be done for the good of the Numoi. I wish no one harm, but we must have Tenon back. Please tell that to your people."

Bacquier bowed formally and left. Natasha, looking pale and worried, hurried after him.

Zanla watched them depart, suddenly very tired. It was done now. He was risking his crew's lives on an insight. It had worked so far, but there was so much further to go.

And how could he feel any confidence, when success depended on interpreting the motivations and reactions of this alien race, and how could he be sure that insights had any value when dealing with such creatures?

And how far, finally, would he go, if the three days went by and Tenon was not returned? What would he do if his bluff was called?

He remembered going back to see Elial after his first Voyage, disgraced, despairing, in need of sympathy and advice. And Elial had said to him, "Success is easy for the Numoi. The true test of greatness lies in living nobly with failure."

Elial, of course, had never made the Council. He was not right for the times, not practical enough in a pragmatic era. Zanla had tried to live by Elial's advice and example. He had done what he had to do, worked his way back. And, when the moment had come, Master at last of his own Ship and his own destination, he had spun the *retheo* far past the safe settings, out to where no Master had ever dared go. And he had been successful beyond his hopes: not only was his career saved, they would find it virtually impossible to keep him off the Council when he presented the volumes of notes, the books and the artifacts, and said, "Here is the race the Ancients sought for. Here is what you sent me to find."

But that dream would only come true if Tenon was returned, if his bluff worked.

It hadn't failed yet, he reminded himself. And if it did fail, there would be other insights, other plans. He had come too far to be stopped now.

17

Ashanti listened carefully. He always listened carefully. When Bacquier was finished he was silent for a moment as he weighed the matter. Then he spoke abruptly. "Can they do it, Professor Aronson?"

"Are they capable of carrying out Zanla's threat, do you mean?"

"Of course."

It was Aronson's turn to be silent. "There are two questions," he said finally. "First, do they have the weapons? My opinion on that would be no, they don't. They've refused to talk specifically about their military capability, but our impression is that it's quite primitive. The second question is: will the destruction of their ship have the consequences Zanla says it will?"

"Precisely," Ashanti murmured.

Aronson's sigh was perfectly audible over the phone. "Well, the fact is, since we have no idea how their ship works, we haven't the slightest basis for saying whether or not Zanla is lying. You'll recall when they first landed this was raised as a consideration against—"

"If I could inject a nonscientific opinion," Bacquier interrupted, "this part of Zanla's threat seems entirely *ad hoc* to me, and for precisely that reason. Why didn't *he* raise this as a consideration at the very beginning, when he still might have doubted our peaceful intentions?"

"That's true," Aronson responded, "but a major determinant of their behavior all along has apparently been the desire to withhold all information from us about the secret of faster-than-light travel. Zanla may be willing to give us this clue only because the alternative—letting us think we could hold on to his missing crew member—is so much more dangerous. He will clearly go to great lengths to get Tenon back."

"Yes, that is very clear," Ashanti said softly. "Thank you, gentlemen. Your opinions are, as ever, valued."

He hung up and made a list of people to be called. None of the calls would be pleasant, he was sure. And the first was not likely to be the easiest. He dialed the number for Pope Clement.

It took some time to get through; his name did not open all doors. He was patient, however, and eventually he heard Clement's distant, tired voice. "I was thinking perhaps I'd get a call from you."

"Yes, you are among the unlucky group."

"Are you going to add your voice to the chorus demanding we give Tenon up?"

"I would not presume to make any demands of you, Holiness. I only wanted to relay some new information that may be useful to you in considering the situation. May I?"

"I am not opposed to listening."

Ashanti told him.

As anticipated, Clement was silent at first, mulling the news. When he spoke, his voice seemed charged with more energy than before. "Pardon me for being blunt, Mr. Ashanti, but why should I believe you? The UN told the world yesterday that Tenon will not be harmed if he is returned to the Numoi. We both know that is a lie. Why should you be telling the truth today?"

"I assure you that it is true," Ashanti replied, unruffled. "My usefulness is at an end in this job if people cannot trust me. To show my good faith in this matter, I will admit to you that there is considerable doubt as to whether the Numoi can do what they threaten. However, there is no doubt that news of their threat will cause considerable unrest, not to say panic, in the world."

"And you will be telling the world, I suppose?"

"Well, certainly it is my duty to inform the various heads of state whose nations might be affected by this. They must have a chance to take whatever steps they feel might be necessary."

"Including whatever persecution of the Catholic Church they feel might induce me to give in, I suppose."

"It would be duplicitous of me to say otherwise, your Holiness. They will do what they can to protect their people. That is the way of the world."

"Well, it was thoughtful of you to give us this news so quickly. It is much preferable to finding out from *L'Osservatore Romano*."

"And may I ask if you intend to act on the information?"

"Not at present, Mr. Ashanti. We are not yet quite ready to yield our principles."

Ashanti smiled. "Very well, your Holiness. I am sure we will speak again."

Odd, he thought, as he stared at his list. Clement's behavior in this situation just could not have been predicted. Was there a new power behind the throne? Was the Pope perhaps becoming a bit senile? No, this was not a throwback to his childhood, but to—what?—ten, fifteen years ago.

Not too many men have ended civil wars single-handedly. They're not easy to end in any manner; Ashanti knew from experience. But Archbishop Herbert had done it, and all his actions since then had to be interpreted with that in mind. Of course it hadn't been a big civil war—a few hundred discontented blacks trying to stir the slumbering masses against a government slowly sinking under the weight of its own ineptitude. But the blacks were smart and desperate and well-armed (by the IRA, still involved in a struggle that not even God could end, it seemed), and their opposition was weary, tentative, afraid. Before a coherent policy had been formed, scores had been killed and the blacks had control of a ten-block area of East London. And, more important, they possessed an atom bomb.

The siege that developed had paralyzed the nation and almost destroyed it. All attempts at negotiation had been fruitless, until one morning Archbishop Herbert walked into the blacks' territory and offered himself in exchange for a peaceful settlement. The offer was spurned, but somehow, through hours of discussions with Kuntasha, the black leader, agreements were reached, concessions were made. By the end of the day a set of proposals had been sent to the Prime Minister; by the end of the week the war was over.

These matters are never very tidy. Afterward, there were questions and recriminations on both sides. The Prime Minister's party was defeated in the next general election, a disaffected West Indian tried to assassinate Kuntasha. But the creaky mechanism of civilized discourse had started up again, and Herbert alone was responsible for that. Ashanti recalled someone asking the Archbishop on television how he had done it. Ill at ease, embarrassed, he had simply shrugged and said, "The Holy Spirit was with me."

Well, perhaps. Certainly there had been little evidence of great diplomatic skill since then. Ashanti himself had bested the Pope on one or two minor matters in the four years of his reign. But it would be dangerous to underestimate a man like Clement. Obviously he was the kind who rose to occasions when one least expected it. And this, evidently, was an occasion to which he was rising.

A foolish, irritating action. Ashanti's most basic instinct was to compromise, to placate, to pacify. And now Clement was forcing him to increase tensions, to anger people, to provoke bitterness. God save him from fanatics.

He picked up the phone and put through a call to the White House. President Gibson would not be very pleased. No one would be very pleased.

18

Harry Stokes was tired and grouchy. More grouchy than tired: he didn't like being chewed out, especially when he hadn't done anything wrong. McMurtry was getting heat from the big shots back in New York, and was simply passing it along. Okay, no hard feelings, but you couldn't expect a person to be exactly jumping for joy over it.

Stokes had spent the previous evening tracking down cabdrivers, limo drivers, bus drivers, anyone who might have picked up passengers from United Flight 407 out of New York City. No one could remember a big Italian and a short something-or-other. Then he had checked the guest registers at a few grungy motels off the Strip. No way he'd get the Sands or the Riviera. Up at the crack of dawn, and McMurtry has the bright idea: if we can't find those two, let's track down the rest of the passengers. See if they have anything to add.

So Stokes was trudging from hotel to hotel with a passenger list in hand, having absolutely no luck at that either, and every time he called in McMurtry was getting nastier. Talk about your glamorous jobs.

At his fifth stop he got lucky. It was a second-rate place downtown, with a nosy desk clerk and faded carpeting. Sure enough, there was Mr. Arthur Hanson of Scarsdale, row 14, seat 9. With an asterisk next to his name on the list. Bernardi had been assigned seats 7 and 8. Well, all right.

Stokes zipped up to the seventh floor and knocked on Mr. Hanson's door. And again, loudly. Finally there was a shuffling of feet and a suspicious eye at the peephole. "Who's't?"

Stokes held up his ID. "I'd just like to ask a few questions, if you don't mind, sir. It won't take long."

"I haven't done nothin'."

"Yes, sir. This investigation has nothing to do with you personally."

"Well, okay."

The bolt slid and the door opened to reveal a rumpled-looking man in a terry-cloth robe. Stokes noticed an empty bottle of Canadian Club sticking out of a wastebasket.

"Had a little party here last night," Mr. Hanson explained.

"Yes, sir. I'd like to talk to you about your plane ride from New York."

"Oh, uh, okay. Good flight. I forget the movie."

"That's all right. I'd like to know if you can remember anything about the people who sat next to you."

Hanson ran his fingers through his thinning hair and scrunched his face up to show how hard he was trying. "Next to me . . . um . . . okay. Nice couple. Italian, I think. First time they'd taken a plane. That was kinda odd."

Stokes shook his head. "Perhaps on the other side of you."

"Other side?" Hanson asked, thinking even harder. "I don't . . . I mean, I had a window seat. There *wasn't* another side."

Stokes digested this. "Perhaps you had better describe this Italian couple."

"Well, the guy was, you know, middle-aged, regular height, kind of Italian-looking. The woman was, I don't know, shorter. Italian-looking too. I think."

Stokes produced a picture. "Is this the man?"

Hanson studied the photo. "Well, the guy wasn't a priest, you know."

"The face, though."

"Oh well, I don't know. I don't think so. Could be."

Stokes sighed. "This couple sat next to you for the whole trip? No changing of seats?"

"No, I don't think so. I mean, it was a couple of days ago, you know?"

Stokes nodded. "Thank you, Mr. Hanson. Will you be staying at this hotel for the next few days?"

"Yup. I'm on vacation. I'd be stayin' in a better place, you know, but—"

"Yes, sir." Stokes departed quickly, not eager to hear anything about the guy's life.

Back in his car, Stokes immediately called in and got hold of McMurtry. He reported what Hanson had told him.

"That's really odd," McMurtry said. "We got a positive ID from a travel agent in New York. Bernardi bought the tickets."

"Well, Bernardi had no way of knowing when we'd be onto him," Stokes pointed out. "Maybe he figured he'd better get himself and the alien into disguises as soon as possible."

"All right, but where does that leave us? We've already checked the hotel registers for Bernardi's handwriting."

"That's true. But I wonder how carefully we checked for *couples*. And let's face it, it's not that hard to alter your handwriting enough to fool an amateur."

"So what do we do? Track down all the couples who registered the day before yesterday?"

"How about all the *Italian* couples? If this guy is as smart as he seems, he wouldn't want to draw attention to himself by putting down O'Toole or something as his name when he looks like he just landed from Naples."

"Good point, and also the ones who didn't have advance reservations, since Bernardi couldn't very well have planned this thing very far ahead of time. Why don't you take Territory One, as we diagrammed it yesterday. I'll coordinate the rest. Maybe we're getting somewhere, eh, Harry?"

"No telling." At least he wasn't getting chewed out.

He spent the next couple of hours working his way along the Strip, rechecking registers. There was a Mr. and Mrs. Vitello from New Rochelle at the Sahara, but they turned out to be bright-eyed newlyweds. Anthony and Florence Gianelli, at Caesar's Palace, were nowhere to be found, but a bellhop remembered them as being in their late sixties and tiny.

At the Holiday Inn a couple fit the bill: Peter and Cynthia Cerullo, New York City. Reservations made the day they arrived. The handwriting on the registration card was sloppy, childish; it could have been disguised. Stokes thought it prudent to call in first. Then he went up to the Cerullos' room. No answer.

Stokes pondered for a moment, and decided it was worth his while to find the manager. Ten minutes later he was inside the room, while the nervous manager stood by, fussing and fretting over this highly irregular procedure. "You don't have a search warrant," he said, having a legalistic turn of mind. "If you arrest them it'll never stand up in court."

That was none of the manager's business, so Stokes didn't tell him they were only interested in capturing, which was what McMurtry said was the word from on high. Instead he quickly examined the bureau, the closet, the suitcases, the bathroom.

His rapid search led to one obvious conclusion: if Bernardi had disguised the alien as a woman, he had sure gone whole hog. Panty hose, bras, slips, perfume, cream rinse, nail polish, disposable douche: it certainly *looked* like a woman was staying in this room. The disposable douche was what really got to Stokes. That seemed to be carrying verisimilitude a bit too far. He made a note to check back later, in case nothing else broke. "That oughta do it," he said to the manager, and turned to go.

A man and a woman were standing in the doorway. "What the hell are you guys doing in our room?" the man demanded.

His voice was tinged with fear, though, and Stokes smoothly took command of the situation. He held his identification out to them and said in a reassuring tone: "My name is Henry Stokes, special agent for the Federal Bureau of Investigation, and this is your hotel manager, Mr., uh, Simpson. I'm sorry we had to enter these premises without your permission, but I'm in the middle of a case that has great importance for national security and you fit a certain basic description of people we would like to question. I hope you will excuse the intrusion."

Stokes was about to take his leave when something about

the couple's attitude made him pause. It was the wife, actually, a short sharp-looking woman with teased blond hair. She should have been looking at *me*, Stokes thought. I'm the intruder. Instead she was looking at her husband, a disgusted, aggrieved expression on her face. Why was she mad at her husband?

"You and your friends," she muttered under her breath.

Noted. "Were you people by any chance on United Flight 407 out of New York City the day before yesterday?"

Mr. Cerullo looked distinctly uncomfortable. He was middle-aged and overweight. There were beads of sweat on his forehead. "What if we were?" he asked with halfhearted belligerence.

"Would you be acquainted with a priest by the name of Albert Bernardi?"

"Oh, for God's sake, let's stop all this nonsense," Mrs. Cerullo said. She walked into the room and sat down on the bed. "We didn't do anything wrong. There's nothing you can arrest us for."

"Perhaps you'd better tell me exactly what you've done, Mrs. Cerullo."

"It's him," she replied, gesturing contemptuously at her husband. "He gets a call from this old friend. 'Hey Pete, you've never been anywhere. Why don't you take a few days off, you and the wife go anywhere you want and I'll buy the plane tickets?' So what if the guy's a priest? There's gotta be a catch, right? Don't do it, I tell him, you'll just get mixed up in something. But no. Pete here has to drop everything and go to Las Vegas so he could lose money at blackjack."

"I didn't see you stayin' at home," Mr. Cerullo remarked from the doorway.

"And before you know it," she went on, ignoring him, "this priest is on the front page of every paper in the country, and the FBI's after Petey here because Bernardi's name is on the tickets. Some friend."

"Don't you knock Bernardi," Cerullo said hotly, advancing toward his wife. "I've known him a hell of a lot longer than I've known you, and he's done a hell of a lot more for me. And just to set the record straight, he told me exactly why he wanted me to take this trip, and I was happy to help him out. I didn't bother telling you because then you wouldn't have come, you'd have blabbed to the police like you blabbed just now."

"Well this is all very interesting," Stokes said, cutting off what he was sure would have been a savage retort from Mrs. Cerullo. "However, my job is to find Bernardi. Would either of you happen to know where he is?"

The husband and wife glared at each other. "I'd tell you if I knew," the wife said.

"Even if I knew I wouldn't tell you," the husband said.

Stokes sighed. "Maybe you'd both better come with me." He'd bring them down to the office and make it all formal, but he doubted that there was more to be gleaned from these two.

He wondered how McMurtry would react. They'd cracked their part of the case, but it hadn't exactly given the big shots what they wanted. He didn't really envy those big shots; this guy Bernardi was not going to just turn up on their doorstep.

That was their problem, though.

19

They all stood when Clement entered, even the ones crippled with age and arthritis, even the ones who despised him. Such was the respect for his office, if not for the man who held it. He motioned for everyone to sit and moved to the head of the table. "I understand that you are all informed of the events up through yesterday," he said in Latin. No one voiced any disagreement. "Good. Perhaps Cardinal Fontanelli will bring you up to date on the latest developments. Carlo?"

Fontanelli stubbed out his cigarette and shifted a few papers. When he began to speak, it was in a raspy monotone; his eyes remained focused on the papers. "The Numoi are threatening to blow up major cities of the world unless Tenon is returned to them. More precisely, they are threatening to threaten this in—well, now it would be two days. The Secretary-General of the United Nations informed his Holiness of this last night. His Holiness refused to order Father Bernardi to release Tenon. Mr. Ashanti then informed some heads of state. It's not certain how many.

"At nine o'clock last night, Washington time, Cardinal O'Dwyer, our Papal Legate to the United States, was summoned to the White House. He was handed a note, which he promptly transmitted to us. The gist of it is that, if Tenon is not produced by noon today, Washington time, President Gibson will hold a press conference in which he will make public the alien threat and will specifically place the blame for all consequences of this on the shoulders of his Holiness. Cardinal O'Dwyer's comments accompanied the note. He said that if his Holiness had been present last night President Gibson would gladly have strangled him.

128

He also mentions that if the press conference is held he expects a lot of broken stained-glass windows by nightfall. Cardinal O'Dwyer is, of course, known for his bluntness."

Fontanelli lit another cigarette. No one spoke. He continued. "We received a cable this morning from Premier Chang of the People's Republic of China, informing us that as of tomorrow all church personnel will be expelled from that country. Unless Tenon is returned.

"Prime Minister Delon of Canada informs us that he will be introducing a bill in Parliament to remove the Church's tax-exempt status. Secretary Gruschenko of the Soviet Union intends to declare Catholics enemies of the state, with appropriate penalties attached. There are several other such messages. I will not bore you with them."

Again there was silence, broken this time by Clement. "Thank you, Carlo. My beloved friends and advisers, I seek your guidance."

The dozen or so men around the table shifted, stared at their hands, sipped their water. "Is it not true that the UN says Tenon will not be harmed if he is returned?" Cardinal LaCroix asked from the far end of the table.

Clement inclined his head. "That is true, they have said that. You perhaps have not seen the videotape of Angela Summers, Jean? The Chitlanians present a basic threat to the Numoi's civilization, similar to that which Christianity posed to ancient Rome. The Numoi cannot afford to show Chitlanians mercy. Tenon's fear appeared to Angela Summers to be real and deep and well-founded. The UN is lying. What other choice do they have?"

"It seems we should look to our own choices," Cardinal Capelli intoned, shifting his massive bulk slightly so as to face Clement. It was the general opinion that, if Capelli had not had the taint of the Curia upon him, he would have been elected Pope instead of Clement. "I for one cannot understand at all why we have not already handed that creature back to whoever owns it."

"Is there not a question of morality involved?" Clement asked mildly.

"Bah. If one looks hard enough there is a question of morality under every rock. The Vatican owns stock in many companies. Must we spend our days and nights studying the morality of every transaction these companies undertake? If we did we would have precious little time left for running the Church."

"Yes, but this question rather appears to have been dropped in our laps," Cardinal Nobuta observed, smiling ingratiatingly in case anyone took offense at his comment.

"It is only a problem because we have turned it into one," Capelli replied dismissively. "Why could we not just have rendered unto Caesar and stayed out of a mess that could do no one any good?"

"Except, perhaps, Tenon," Cardinal LaCroix remarked.

"And who is this Tenon?" Capelli asked, his voice rising so that it dominated the room. "Have our theologians determined that these aliens have souls, so that we should worry about what happens to them? If this creature does have a soul—and I am willing to grant it—why is his safety worth more than the well-being of the one true Church founded by Jesus Christ? One is not morally required to endanger one's own life to save another's. I think that principle could be applied here."

"But in our case we are talking about stained-glass windows, not lives, are we not?" inquired Nobuta, still smiling.

"Speak to me after the riots start, your Eminence," Capelli countered.

"Now let us be calm, Giovanni," Cardinal Erhard said. "We are here to advise, not vent our anger."

"Then here is my advice, Klaus: to save face, publicly ask Ashanti for further clarification about Tenon's safety. Ashanti will clarify. Restate the Church's views on relations with the aliens, declare that we are satisfied Tenon will be fairly treated, and hand him over to the UN."

"Sounds like somebody's solution for the American involvement in the Vietnam War," Cardinal Bolger commented. "Declare that we've won and pull out."

"What is our alternative?"

Bolger shrugged. "Perhaps," he offered, "it would not be so bad for the Church, to go through an experience like this. Strength through adversity, you know."

"You may be right," Erhard replied. "Perhaps we will be admired for the purity of our purpose. But that all depends on how our action is perceived: as an example of heroic moral courage, or as an instance of pitifully misplaced priorities. To my way of thinking it would be a great deal of both. If such an ambivalent reaction is widespread, I doubt that the Church will thrive as a result."

"Oh, I'm not speaking of growth. I'm speaking of purification."

"Purification," Capelli snorted. "The eternal hope: that a good dose of persecution will solve all our problems. If only Diocletian were emperor again, we would all be saints."

"At least we wouldn't be worried about the growth rate of our investment portfolio," Nobuta remarked, his smile widening into a grin.

Capelli was about to reply, but Clement's raised hand forestalled him. "Thank you, Eminences. There appear to be two courses of action suggested: the present one, and that of our esteemed colleague Cardinal Capelli. It would be useful for us to see how many favor each. If no one has any objections, would those of you who support the present policy please raise your hands?"

Three tentative hands. Clement looked around the table. "You may vote too, if you wish, Anthony," he said to Collingwood, who was busy taking notes in the far corner.

Collingwood looked up at Clement. "Yes, your Holiness," he responded. He did not move.

Clement waited until it was clear there was no misunderstanding. "And those who favor Cardinal Capelli's position?" he whispered finally.

Ten hands. Including Collingwood's.

Clement appraised the faces of those arrayed against him, and abruptly stood up. "Thank you all," he said quickly. "We shall pray on this matter now." He rose and strode hurriedly out of the room.

After a brief moment of silence the meeting broke up, the cardinals departing in twos and threes to gossip and speculate. Collingwood remained seated, staring at his notes. Fontanelli came up to him on the way out. "That certainly was a surprising moment," he remarked.

"Circumstances change, your Eminence," Collingwood said, not looking up. "The wise man changes with them."

"Indeed. You are well on your way to wisdom, then. Of

course he won't go along with us. He's committed himself. It would be a pity if you were finally to achieve wisdom, and find yourself out of a job in which to exercise it."

"Perhaps part of wisdom is knowing when that doesn't matter."

"Indeed. Good luck, Monsignor."

"Thank you, your Eminence."

20

A lesser woman would have become discouraged by now, and when Madeleine West stopped to think about it (which was not often), she did have to admit to an occasional moment of uncertainty. The Las Vegas fiasco hadn't helped, of course, nor had the rather snappish conversation with Fitzgerald that morning. All the leads were petering out, the legwork was uncovering nothing, the phoned-in tips were all from crackpots . . . and now the Numoi were threatening to blow the world up, so the President said. *That* didn't do anything to lessen the pressure on her.

The best approach, of course, was not to think about such matters. Just do your job, and save the worrying for later. And perhaps eventually the phone will ring. . . .

"Mrs. Bernardi on line 7."

"Thank you, Sheila." She took a deep breath, and picked up the receiver. "Madeleine West here."

"Have you found Albert yet?" the woman asked. She sounded afraid.

"No, ma'am."

"No, I guess he's too smart for you. You'd never find him, unless . . ."

"Yes, Mrs. Bernardi?"

"Come see me, would you? Alone."

"I'll be right over."

She was there in twenty minutes. Mrs. Bernardi was wearing a blue print dress that was too young for her. Her makeup could not conceal her red-rimmed eyes. "Do you understand this blowing up cities?" she asked as soon as West had sat down.

"I understand that this is very serious business."

133

"But will they actually do it? The President seemed to think maybe it was a bluff."

"You really know as much about it as I do, Mrs. Bernardi. The point President Gibson was making, I guess, is that we can't just assume it's a bluff, even if it is."

"Yes, I suppose. It's so frightening. Why did it have to come to this?"

West just shook her head in sympathy.

"And the Pope," Mrs. Bernardi went on. "You'd think he—oh, I don't know. There are lives at stake. Human lives."

"Your son's life," West noted.

"Yes. And not the Pope's." There was bitterness in her voice. She stared off into the distance—at some favorite photograph of her son, West imagined. Her knuckles showed white on the arms of her wing chair.

Now, West thought. "We are prepared to offer clemency to your son if you help us find him," West said. "He will not be charged with any offense he may have committed in this episode."

Mrs. Bernardi brightened, then looked dubious. "How do I know you have that authority?"

West shrugged and removed her phone from her pocket. She dialed a number and turned up the volume of the receiver.

"Good afternoon, FBI."

"Good afternoon. Mr. Fitzgerald's office, please."

A pause. "Director's office."

"Hello, this is Madeleine West. I would like to speak to Mr. Fitzgerald, please. It is a matter of extreme importance."

"One moment, Ms. West."

Another pause. "Madeleine, what's up?"

"Mr. Fitzgerald, I'm with Albert Bernardi's mother in her apartment. I have just been assuring her that the government will take no action against Father Bernardi should he be found as a result of information supplied by her. Can you confirm that this will be our policy?"

"I certainly can. Is Mrs. Bernardi listening?"

"Yes sir, yes I am," Mrs. Bernardi replied.

"Good. Mrs. Bernardi, I am the Director of the Federal

Bureau of Investigation. I want to assure you that we have no interest in prosecuting your son for anything he may have done. We just want to hand this alien over to his people and get the world back to normal again. You know, I'm a staunch Catholic, and like a lot of Catholics I've been disappointed with the Pope's attitude in all of this. I've got to admire your son, and I respect his sense of obedience to the Pope, but you have to admit that things have gotten out of hand."

"Yes, you're right, they have."

"Well, is there any other assurance I can give you?"

"No, uh, it was very good of you to talk with us, sir."

"Well, great. I hope you make the right decision. Madeleine, you keep in touch. You're doing a fine job."

West put away her phone.

Mrs. Bernardi looked solemn and impressed, but still unhappy. "Why did this ever have to happen?" she whispered.

West reached out and covered Mrs. Bernardi's hand with her own. "I know it's hard," she said.

Mrs. Bernardi looked down at the floor. "He called me when he got into town the other day. Said he didn't want me to be worried, but people might be looking for him. I didn't know what he meant, of course, but I asked him where he would be. He was a bit reluctant at first, but finally he told me."

She took a deep breath. "He had a girl friend in high school. Her name's Jenny Salieri. She has a place somewhere out on Long Island. She's an artist. He said he'd be staying there. It's a cottage. I was a little shocked, you know, but he said it would be all right, she wasn't using it. I don't know. Things are so confusing. I don't know what—"

"Do you happen to have the address, Mrs. Bernardi?"

She shook her head, and as she did the tears came pouring out. "He'll never forgive me," she sobbed.

"Of course he will," West said. "Don't worry about a thing," she added as she headed for the door.

"Salieri?" Dewey said. "Hold on. Yeah. Here it is. Jennifer Salieri. We talked to her. Has a Manhattan address listed. Must be a summer cottage. She said she corresponded a bit with Bernardi since he went into the Jesuits, but hasn't seen him in ten years. Nothing suspicious. She's a fashionable artist, it says here. Into holography and that sort of thing. Don't understand any of it myself."

"Get the address of the cottage," West said. "And make sure Mrs. Bernardi's apartment is covered."

It took them fifteen minutes to track the address down, and West was on her way, with two carloads of agents following. They got explicit directions over the phone from the local police, and within the hour they were around the corner from the cottage.

"Surround it," West ordered. "Stay out of sight. I'll go in."

It was twilight as they advanced toward the cottage. The neighborhood was poshly rural. Bernardi has rich friends, West thought. They could hear the roar of the ocean, but it was just out of sight beyond the dunes. The evening was clear and cold.

There was a light on in the cottage. Excellent. The agents fanned out expertly. West looked around. No car. No way of escaping. She walked up to the door and knocked.

No answer. She stood and listened. No sounds. She tried the knob. The door was open. She entered.

Fancy, she thought. Dark-stained wood and expensive orientals. A large picture window looking out on the ocean. Strange, free-standing art objects, all curves and colors. For once she agreed with Dewey: she couldn't make sense out of any of that stuff, either. She closed the door behind her.

A quick search showed that the place was empty, but that someone had been there quite recently. The ashes in the fireplace were still giving off heat; a dirty frying pan in the sink was half filled beneath a dripping faucet.

There was no trace of men's clothing in the closet, though; nothing to suggest it was her prey who had lived here. Had Mrs. Bernardi lied to her? Not likely. Had she changed her mind and called her son to let him know they were on their way? But the phone was tapped: if her agents had fouled up . . .

Her telecom buzzed urgently. She switched it on. "West."

"Someone's walking up the beach. Looks like he's heading for the house."

"Keep your positions. Let him enter."

She stood by the fireplace, out of sight of the back door. After a few moments she heard the familiar sequence of sounds: feet on steps, key being inserted, creak of door opening, bang of it shutting. The light went on in the kitchen, and a dark figure moved back and forth. There was the sound of running water. Doing the dishes. West moved forward.

She took out her identification and her revolver. She walked into the kitchen. "FBI. Don't move, please."

The figure didn't move.

"Turn around."

The figure turned. It was a woman. She was smiling. "May I at least put the frying pan down?" she inquired.

West nodded. She felt depressed and frustrated. "Jennifer Salieri?"

"Yes, of course. And who are you?"

She felt something more than frustration. Envy. Yes, stupid envy. Jenny Salieri must have been—what?—close to forty, but she was still darkly beautiful. And elegant, even in the casual slacks and sweater. West thought of the diet she had long ago given up on, the clothes she didn't have the time to coordinate. Damn, this case was really getting on her nerves. "My name is Madeleine West. We received information that people we are looking for might be in this house."

"Al Bernardi and friend, right? Let's sit down, shall we? Can I get you a drink?"

Feeling foolish, West lowered the revolver, but ignored the pleasantries. "Would you tell me what you know about this matter?"

"Well, as you can see, they're not here. And I honestly have no idea where they are."

"But you know more than you told the agent who spoke to you earlier."

Salieri leaned back against the sink. "Oh, I suppose I should be brutally frank, although it won't get you anywhere. Al called me a few days ago—just before this business broke in the papers—and asked for a favor. Well, I could never refuse Al anything, although he refused me often enough. It was really nothing. He said that people were going to be looking for him, and there was a good chance they would think he was at this cottage. Did I mind, was all he wanted to know. Well, of course not. I invited him to use the place if he wanted to, but he said no, he had other plans."

"He didn't mention what those plans were, did he?"

She smiled and shook her head. "I'm afraid not. And if he had I'm sure it would have been a lie that'd take you another day or two to unravel. He'll end up confusing you so much that when you actually do find him you won't be sure it's for real. He's just about the cleverest man I know. What a waste. Are you sure you won't have that drink?"

West pondered the information. She could be lying. They could actually have been here and she was covering for them. It wouldn't hurt to run a check on the area. They wouldn't turn up, though. West knew in her bones that the woman was telling the truth. And that bastard had lied to his mother. West was getting a headache. "I'm sorry. I don't have the time. If you think of anything that might help us, please give us a call. We're not interested in Bernardi. We just want the alien back."

The woman shrugged. "Sure. If you find Al—which I doubt—say hi from me, will you?"

West nodded. Now she was carrying messages to him. Outside, in the darkness, a wave of anger swept over her—at him, at the woman, but mostly at herself, for feeling that stab of envy, for letting the case affect her emotions.

It occurred to her that she had little reason to envy Jenny Salieri, who had obviously spent her life longing for a man who preferred to be celibate. That must be a pretty tough thing to live with.

Enough. She gave her orders and headed home.

21

Clement sat in his office reading Cardinal Newman. He had made a few calls, but they had been depressing; he had tried to do some mundane paperwork, but had been unable to concentrate. Now it was evening, his back was aching, all deadlines had passed, and he was alone.

At the best of times his job was lonely; at the worst it was as if he inhabited his own planet, and his only human contacts were the flickering shadows of a TV screen, portraying an existence so far removed from his own that it could hardly be considered real. I did not ask to live on this planet, he thought (not for the first time), but that was self-pity. When Pusateri had hobbled up to him after the balloting in the Conclave and put the question to him, he had whispered "*Accepto*"—and he had known what he was accepting. He had chosen, and this was the fruit of his choice.

There was a knock on the door. Clement smiled. His isolation, after all, was mental and emotional; hardly physical. "Yes?" he murmured.

It was Collingwood. He had been expecting him, really. There was something to be worked out between them. "Come in, Anthony."

Collingwood walked across the room and sat down in silence. He didn't know where to start, clearly. How often had he been at a loss for words in his life? In a way Clement pitied him. It was an awkward position for an ambitious man like him to be in. Still, it was all his own doing, and Clement had more important things to worry about.

The problem was, Clement realized, that he didn't much like Collingwood. The man was brilliant; he had made himself indispensable, really; he was, for all Clement could tell, a good man, a good priest; his motives always seemed to be worthy, his positions were always Christian. And yet he seemed cold and manipulative; one could not laugh with him, for example. His laughter had to have a point, had to accomplish something. He lacked the fire of the Holy Spirit. He made Clement uncomfortable.

Such reactions were not sinful perhaps, but they were certainly not laudable. If Collingwood caught any hint of them, it was not from lack of effort on Clement's part to suppress them. Anthony was a child of God, one of his flock. Also, Clement needed him (just as he needed Clement). All other considerations were superfluous.

"You look worried, Anthony."

"I've been watching the news," Collingwood replied pointedly.

"Yes. Riots in Mexico City. Nuns attacked in Bangkok. A stony silence from the Vatican."

"Matters will only get worse if the silence continues."

"The Church has suffered before. It has sometimes done her good."

"Surely it suffered to more purpose than this."

"You seemed to feel before that this was rather important." Clement raised his hand to stop Collingwood's reply. "No, let me see if I can say it for you. Circumstances have changed. What may have deserved our support before no longer outweighs other considerations. The stakes have been raised. Our bluff has been called. Is that about right?"

"I didn't know your Holiness was acquainted with gambling terminology."

Clement smiled. "I am perhaps acquainted with more than you give me credit for, Anthony."

"Well, your analysis is correct, of course. I simply don't see why you won't accept it. Cardinal Capelli is obnoxious—I suppose I'm obnoxious—but that shouldn't obscure the truth of what we say."

"You are owed an explanation, I suppose," Clement responded. "I doubt that any I give will satisfy you, though. I see this, purely and simply, as a moral issue. Ultimately political concerns—and all other concerns—must yield to morality. I am willing to accept the burden of these other concerns."

"But the creature isn't human! It will take the theologians years to sort out the moral issues involved. Why risk so much on an unproved case?"

"To me it is not unproved. Let the theologians ponder as long as they want. I feel the obligation."

Collingwood sighed. He half rose from his chair, then slumped back down in it. He looked decidedly uncomfortable.

"I give you permission to say whatever you want," Clement said mildly. "I will not take offense at it. I will not let it affect your standing with me."

"Thank you, Holiness," Collingwood whispered. He stared at Clement intently for a moment, then got up and began to pace the room. He stopped in front of the window, turned, and spoke. "What I fear," he said, "is that you perceive this as the Race War all over again. That you finally feel you have found an issue you can summon up your courage and fight for. That a personal crisis is obscuring the reality of the situation for you. That you're out to prove something at the expense of the Church."

Clement nodded. "Your fears are not unreasonable. I'm only a man. My motivations cannot be entirely pure. But look at it this way, Anthony: would I do right by my conscience if I were to ignore its promptings, out of fear that my actions would be interpreted as you have interpreted them? I cannot spend my life examining my motivations. Ultimately I must act."

"All right, but you aren't acting! You are letting events carry you. You've got to see that this is wrong. The grandeur of your role in the Race War was that, while everyone else sat around and worried, you *did* something. Sitting in the Apostolic Palace and reading Newman is not the leadership you should be providing the Church."

Clement sighed. Now Collingwood was hitting home. Surely there should be something more—but what? When the world will not listen—when even the people who have taken vows of obedience to you are muttering mutinously. He felt utterly powerless, swept along by the flood of events, waiting for the inevitable. But there was no inevitable, of course. There was free will, and that meant he had some control.

The control could be infinitesimal, certainly. Still, he hadn't really expected to have any effect on Kuntasha. He had been shaving one morning, and the radio had been on, intoning evacuation plans and continued stalemates, and he had suddenly noticed the deep age lines on his face, the yellowed fingernails around the razor, and it was as if he had truly looked at himself for the first time in a decade. And the decade had not been kind to him. The thought of death lodged in his mind like a pebble in his shoe, digging into him at every step. But a lifetime of prayer and meditation had prepared him to accept the idea of death, so almost immediately he thought: yes, I am going to die. What will I do with my life? And at that instant he was prepared to walk past the rifles and offer what was left of himself for peace. If he were rejected, things would not be any worse. If he were killed—well, it was not an ignominious way to die. If he succeeded . . .

Well, he had succeeded. And here he sat. Older, but hardly wiser, seeking to recapture something he wasn't sure he ever really had. He looked at his fingernails. Still yellow. Nothing had really changed.

And the answer came to him. "You are right, Anthony. This is no time for sitting. Get me Ashanti on the phone. I want to talk to the alien leader."

Collingwood stared at him, clearly struggling to make sense of this. "You want to go to their ship?" he asked.

"I can hardly invite him to come here, can I?"

Collingwood found himself walking south from the Vatican, through Trastevere. The streets were narrow and cobblestoned, without sidewalks. They twisted and curved and doubled back on themselves; he was quickly lost in them, and more than once had to jump out of the way of taxis that were just as lost as he was. No matter.

He had never been in this section of Rome before. There was really no reason for him to come here. The Trasteverini, he had heard, claimed to be the most Roman of the Romans. Your family had to have lived here for generations before you were accepted by them. He was an outsider. Always had been—even in college, in America. Even at the seat of power—he was a foreigner, a schemer, treated with mistrust and fear, making his way alone, friendless.

He passed the warm glow of a tavern. Inside they were shouting out some bawdy song, laughing and clinking glasses. He raised the collar of his coat; he wouldn't have minded getting drunk, but how could he manage it? It would have to be alone, in his room in the Apostolic Palace—a ludicrous thought. He walked on.

Clement wanted to meet with Zanla. Ashanti was trying to arrange it now. They could be on their way as soon as tomorrow. Headlines around the planet. Hopes raised in billions of breasts. Clement had done it before, after all. . . .

No matter what Clement said about moral obligations, it was clear to Collingwood now that the man was simply out to replicate the great triumph of his life. Perhaps it was unconscious; perhaps he had really convinced himself that he was somehow saving the Church. It really didn't matter. What mattered was that he was going through with it, and Collingwood was powerless to stop him.

What mattered was that Clement hadn't the skill to carry out the mission successfully. There might be some way of presenting his position, some points of compromise that could be worked out, but Clement just wasn't the man for the job. He would be rebuffed, and the riots would continue, and they would be one day closer to total chaos.

Damn Bernardi. Why had he ever listened to the man? Why had he allowed himself to be seduced from the principles of caution and prudence that had gotten him where he was? The idea had been stupid from the beginning—to expect to produce some kind of great revival of religion out of this business. If they had gone about it slowly, diplomatically, the impact would not have been as powerful, but at least they might have gotten closer to the truth. As it was, he was implicated in what appeared to be the beginning of interplanetary war.

Collingwood had reached the Tiber. A prostitute brushed up against him and muttered something in Italian. She had orange hair, and her breath smelled of garlic. He pushed past her, feeling suddenly nauseated.

He stood on the bridge but couldn't bring himself to

cross to the east bank. He was not a Roman. There was nothing for him there.

Perhaps this was how Tenon felt, Collingwood thought, standing alone in an alien world. All he had was his religion—and that, ultimately, was all Collingwood had too. Like Tenon, he was willing to go to great lengths to keep his religion from being destroyed.

He strode back to the Vatican, sticking close to the Tiber and main streets. Despite the cold, his palms were wet. Once he was in his room he took a pencil and made out a list of names. Then, without a pause, he called the first name on the list.

"Hello?"

"Hello, is this Father Jeffries?"

"Yes."

"Ed, this is Monsignor Collingwood calling, from the Vatican. Am I interrupting anything?"

"Nothing that can't wait while I talk to the Vatican."

"Yes, that one little word accomplishes a lot in certain circles. Listen, in the Chancery there in New York you're pretty close to what goes on in the Archdiocese, aren't you?"

"I like to think so, certainly."

"Well, I have a rather delicate matter to bring up that might call on your knowledge and your contacts. I hope I can rely on your discretion."

"Certainly you can, Monsignor."

"Fine. You, uh, you are certainly aware of the Pope's position on this alien business."

"Of course."

"Well, things are a little more complicated than they might appear on the newscasts. You see, his Holiness feels that the position he is taking is the only one that would be publicly acceptable for an institution like ours to take. We can't say anything else without lowering our moral stature. On the other hand, he is fully aware of the disastrous consequences if the present state of affairs is allowed to continue."

"It's quite a dilemma."

"It is indeed. Well, the easiest way out of it would simply be for the alien to be found, without the Pope having to turn him in. Unfortunately, the authorities seem to be having no luck in tracking him down. So we have decided, in the strictest secrecy, to try to help them. We don't enjoy doing this, but circumstances are forcing us."

"I understand perfectly."

"Wonderful. What we would like you to do is to make discreet inquiries among your acquaintances, to see if anyone has any information about where Bernardi and Tenon might be. Since Bernardi is from New York, and his car was found there, it seems possible that he is in the city, and he may well have sought aid from one of his clerical friends. You're in as good a position as anyone to find out if this theory is true."

"I will certainly do my best, Monsignor."

"Great. You should not, of course, say anything about this call, or about the Vatican's interest in the matter. Vague hints should be sufficient to make the point."

"I understand. But could I just ask: why isn't Cardinal Rafferty the one to be informed about this? It would seem—"

"It was felt best to keep this effort confined to lower levels of the hierarchy. Deniability, that sort of thing. What would his Eminence do, after all, except turn the matter over to you?"

"That's true, I guess."

"Let me give you my personal phone number. If you learn anything, call me. Any time. A lot depends on it."

"Of course. I'll do my best."

After Collingwood had hung up he lay back and stared at the ceiling for a while. He was soaked with perspiration, he suddenly realized. He longed for a shower. It would take more than a shower to cleanse him now, though. He looked at the second name on the list, and picked up the phone again.

22

Ergentil was filling up sheet after sheet with her grue-some message. It was a boring, futile task, since she knew it was unlikely Zanla would attempt to carry out the threat. For one thing, she knew it was difficult to calibrate the *retheo* that finely; for another, it would only give them an-other couple of days before the next stage of their bluff would have been called. If the aliens didn't turn Tenon over within these three days, nothing was likely to work.

Still, she didn't really mind doing it. It gave her the sense that *something* was being accomplished, and that she had a part in it. She worked at it steadily, until she noticed Zanla standing in the doorway, staring at her. How long had he been there? They seemed incapable of not annoying each other.

"Yes?" she inquired coldly.

"I have just spoken with Bacquier," he said. "It seems the leader of this religion wants to visit me—I suppose to talk us out of our threat."

"How does he expect to do that?"

Zanla gestured his ignorance.

"Did you agree to meet him?"

"I could see no reason not to. Conceivably I could talk *him* into giving up Tenon."

"I'd say neither of you has much chance of success."

"Perhaps."

Ergentil noted the tone. "What do you have in mind?" she demanded.

"Bacquier told me before that this Pope has no military power. Presumably he will come by himself. Presumably we could—"

"No," she interrupted firmly. "The Laws of Hospitality

forbid it. If we accept this man as a guest, we must treat him as a guest."

"That's the schoolbook answer, of course," Zanla countered. "But we aren't in school. If we capture this Pope then surely his followers will have to give up Tenon in exchange for him. Our problem would be solved."

"It is deception."

"What about the threat I made to Bacquier? Wasn't that deception? You approved of that."

"It was different. We weren't dealing with a guest. The Laws of Hospitality—"

"Oh, please don't lecture me. Isn't the law of survival more important?"

"There is no such law," Ergentil responded. She was about to elaborate on his lack of regard for his religion when she felt a sudden, unexpected surge of pity for him. "You wouldn't have come to see me about this if you were at ease in your own mind," she noted.

Zanla glared at her for a moment, then dropped his gaze to the floor. "You have written enough," he said. "I have been talking to Rothra and the other officers. The crew is not in good shape. We could try for one city if necessary. No more."

"And the Pope?"

"We will see what he has to say." Zanla bowed quickly and left the room.

Ergentil gazed after him, a little surprised—at herself, for the sympathy she felt for him; and at Zanla, for agreeing with her so readily. He was not such a bad person, perhaps. He had a flaw, that was all, a flaw that blinded his perceptions and warped his actions. Did he know she knew? It hardly mattered at this point. What mattered was that she try to correct the mistakes that flaw might cause.

She looked down at the mass of useless papers, and wondered what the next step would be.

Bernardi glanced at the headlines as he made himself breakfast. So the Pope was going to call on the Numoi. He approved, he decided as he fried his egg. The status quo wasn't doing anyone any good: himself, among others.

For one thing, he had little to do but eat and sleep, so he

was getting fat. For another, he was bored to death. He had tried reading, with some vague idea of getting through Proust, but he was unable to concentrate, so he ended up mostly watching television and doing crossword puzzles. An outlaw's life is not always an exciting one.

And, of course, the status quo was evidently not too good for the world as a whole, or for the Church. At least so it seemed from reading the newspaper. But he tried not to think much about that as the endless hours passed. That was Clement's business, ultimately, and not his own. The Pope was by no means infallible in matters like this, and everyone agreed he wasn't the Church's greatest intellect— but then again, neither was Bernardi. At a certain point you just have to decide to obey, and to pray.

Bernardi poured himself a cup of coffee, buttered his toast, and sat down to read the paper more thoroughly. This was really the high point of his day—he couldn't deny the pleasure he took in seeing his name in print: "The clever Jesuit continues to elude the authorities," "FBI spokesmen express optimism, but insiders say the Bureau has no real leads as to the whereabouts of Tenon and Bernardi." And so on. He wondered if they'd cracked his mother yet. He'd have to spend some time with her after all of this was over. She would need some reassuring. In the meantime . . .

He heard a stirring in the next room. In the meantime, life was pretty dull. He poured another cup of coffee and brought it to his roommate.

Sabbata was left out of the bonding sessions now. There was no one for her to bond with; she was a useless appendage. The rest of the crew had been solicitous at first, but as they received inklings of the seriousness of the situation she could feel them start to avoid her. Wasn't she partly to blame? Would Tenon have left if she had been a better bondmate? She could feel the questions in their stares. They were questions she had asked herself.

She wandered through the empty corridors, lonely and unhappy and, occasionally, angry. She deserved better, she thought. She had done her job, practiced her religion. Why should life turn out this way for her? But she could not sustain her anger. Someone, she was sure, was bound to be able to explain to her just why things were as they were.

She went to her room—*their* room—and lay down, not caring if this violated regulations. What could they do to her now? And, lying down, she knew what she wanted to do. She went through the brief ritual, then thrust her mind out—out past the walls of the Ship, out into the alien world, seeking her mate wherever he was, needing to know if at least he was alive and happy. She ultimately didn't begrudge him his decision and the problems it had caused everyone. She only wanted to know that *some* good had come of it.

She searched, moving through an emptiness greater than any she had experienced, until finally she found him.

Did he feel it? No, his mind was elsewhere. The rejection was total now. But there was something—

She maintained the fragile bond as long as she could, then let it slip away. Forever. She breathed deeply and closed her eyes. She would never understand, but she was satisfied.

23

The white plane touched down at Logan. It was early evening, and the air was cold. Clement's back ached; he held both railings as he descended to the tarmac. Blue lights were flashing; the noise was deafening; scores of people were waiting, all undoubtedly with crucial reasons for being here—just as he could not travel with less than a planeful of aides and guards and medical people and journalists and assorted hangers-on whose functions he had never ascertained.

He sighed with relief when he saw a large swatch of red approaching. It clarified into Cardinal O'Dea, holding his arms out in greeting. Kiss of ring, and then an embrace: somewhat more than perfunctory; O'Dea had always been a loyal supporter.

"It's good to see you, Holiness," O'Dea said. "You're looking well."

"We look awful, your Eminence. And we feel worse."

"It's been quite a strain, hasn't it?"

"At our age, we should be tending a garden in a rest home, instead of talking in the first person plural and dealing with problems like this."

"Someone must bear the burden."

"Like to try it for a while?"

"No thanks. I've got my own. Cars are waiting, I understand, if we just follow the security people. We will head straight for Greenough."

"Excellent." Clement headed into the terminal with O'Dea and proceeded through a labyrinth of corridors. They chatted amiably about their infirmities, but Clement detected a sense of strain in the cardinal's small talk. Was his own tension as noticeable?

150

Outside, he caught a glimpse of TV cameras and crowds jammed against police barriers. Then he was inside a limousine flanked by motorcycles, and in a few moments they were speeding away from the airport. The route was over highway for a while, then through a long tunnel. When they came out of the tunnel, suddenly they were in the midst of thousands of people pushed up against the barricades in the narrow city streets. Clement was not surprised. He was used to crowds.

But he was not used to the mood of this one. He saw shaking fists and weeping women and faces twisted in anger; he read the hand-lettered signs telling him to get out of Boston and heard the shouts and curses above the wail of the sirens.

Abruptly it was all behind him and the motorcade was racing along highway again. He remained shaken, however. He turned to O'Dea, who was staring uncomfortably over his chins at his folded hands. "I do not understand," he said softly. "In the past—"

"The past is gone, Holiness," O'Dea replied. "Boston is the nearest large city to the aliens. Many people feel that therefore we will be the first to be threatened and attacked. You are the one who can prevent this, but—"

"But I won't."

O'Dea shrugged and continued to stare at his hands.

"What do you think, Martin? You talk of your burden. I must be it. Do you agree with those people?"

O'Dea glanced over at him, and Clement knew he was deciding whether to be diplomatic and smooth it over or tell him the truth. Honesty won. "I admire you, but it's a mistake."

Clement sighed. "You think so too."

O'Dea turned to face Clement. "Seventeen percent fewer communicants last year, twenty-four percent fewer baptisms. Three more parishes closed, most of the rest with just one priest. You know the story. It's the same here as everywhere. Now the people see the Holy Father abandoning them. Even if the city is spared, the people will remember. They'll say you cared more for the one alien than you cared for them."

"Is that how you feel?"

O'Dea's dark eyes burned into him for a moment, then cooled, softened. "They don't know you. I do. There's the difference."

"But you still feel it's a mistake," Clement persisted.

O'Dea nodded solemnly. "I think you are risking the destruction of the Church. I don't think it's worth it."

No reply could be made to that. He gazed out into the gathering darkness as they sped along the highway. The destruction of the Church. Had the man no faith? For two thousand years people had been predicting its destruction, but God had protected it. Could Geoffrey Herbert of London, England, accomplish what emperors and plagues and heretics had failed to do?

He thought back to his days in the London slums. Newly ordained and the whole world to save. Existing on three hours' sleep a night and every minute of those three begrudged. What would Father Herbert have done, he wondered, if in 1957 he had been given this problem to solve? He had been a firm believer in moral courage, of course. But he also saw a moral obligation to reduce the world's suffering. He might well have solved it differently.

One thing would have been the same, though. The child is father to the man. Once he had started on his course, nothing short of God Himself would have made him swerve from it.

Pig-headed stubbornness, or admirable tenacity? Depends on whether you're right or wrong, of course. Father Herbert wouldn't have doubted that he was right. Pope Clement wasn't quite so sure.

His eyes fluttered and closed against the darkness. Too much thinking.

Cardinal O'Dea was prodding him gently. "We have arrived, your Holiness." The Pope squinted out at lights and confusion and, just beyond, the small steeple of a church.

"Most Precious Blood," O'Dea murmured. "The pastor's name is Father Gardner."

"He was involved in this, wasn't he?" Clement wondered. "Are those reporters over there?"

"I believe so," O'Dea replied.

"I will have my secretary give them a statement. I seem to be awfully tired."

"Of course."

O'Dea signaled to the chauffeur, and instantly the doors were open and they were heading past the TV lights into the shabby old rectory. The next few minutes passed in the usual blur of introductions and blessings. The only face he kept in his mind was the pastor's—florid, frightened, with once-intelligent eyes now dull and wary. He too was in this over his head.

As soon as the pleasantries had died down the Pope pleaded weariness and was immediately shown to his room. It was on the second floor, large and drafty, undoubtedly the pastor's own. Marcello was already there, laying out his nightclothes, putting his heating pad in place, arranging his pills.

"Well, how do you like it here, Marcello?"

The valet shrugged noncommittally. "I've been in worse," he replied in Italian.

"But you have gotten used to better."

"Who am I to say I deserve better, though, Holiness?"

Clement smiled and sat down to take off his red slippers. Marcello rushed to help him. How did he deserve Marcello?

Collingwood came in several minutes later, as Clement was about to get into bed. "I spoke to the press," he said. "They were rather hostile."

"Of course. What did you tell them?"

"What could I tell them? Just that you are here to speak with the Numian leader, you hope the discussions will be fruitful, you haven't changed your position. . . ." Collingwood stopped and shifted uncomfortably.

"Yes, you were right: I have not," Clement said, and they both were silent for a while.

When Collingwood replied, it was in a low, rushed tone, like a man rehearsing a speech. "Strike a bargain with him, Holiness. Make him promise not to harm Tenon. Then go on television and tell Bernardi to give Tenon over. The Church has had to compromise all through its history in order to survive. It can compromise now."

Clement sighed. "There is no guarantee of Tenon's safety," he replied gently. "Without a guarantee—"

"You make a judgment, in the absence of a guarantee," Collingwood broke in. "You judge that Zanla can be trusted, so you take the chance and save the world from misery and the Church from ruin."

"You are asking me to be a hypocrite, or a liar."

"I'm asking you to save the Church."

Clement smiled wearily. "The Church may advance through compromise, but not through sin. Get some sleep, Anthony. It's been a long day."

Collingwood stood silently for a moment, until his usual icy self-possession could settle on his features. "As you wish," he murmured, and exited quietly.

Clement sat on the edge of the bed until the door had closed, then switched off the light and got beneath the covers. Outside the room there was a low murmur of voices. The wind rattled the poorly-made window. Clement was cold and lonely. He prayed for a while, then drifted off into a restless, unsatisfying sleep.

In his little cubicle down the hall, Collingwood made no attempt to sleep. He sat rigidly in an uncomfortable ladder-back chair and gazed unseeingly at the dismal backyard of the rectory: snow-encrusted clotheslines, chain-link fence, scrawny bushes, a couple of pine trees swaying in the wind.

One by one he was reviewing the possibilities, assessing the consequences. It was a procedure that was second nature to him by now. He did it out of habit, not from any hope that somehow he would come up with a sequence that would end happily. The ones that did were fantasies, pipe dreams. And the greatest fantasy was that Clement would succeed tomorrow. He hadn't prepared a strategy, he hadn't asked advice, he hadn't studied the Numoi, he hadn't done anything that would give the slightest hope of success. It was clear that he was relying on the Holy Spirit to inspire him in his meeting with Zanla—which sounded very nice, but in Collingwood's experience was just an excuse for not having done what you were supposed to do. When would Clement learn that holiness just wasn't enough, that more was required in his position, and if he didn't have what was required he should turn to those who did?

Collingwood exhaled slowly. The possibilities were exhausted. He had done what he could. Perhaps, like Clement, he should leave things in God's hands now. Perhaps he should resign immediately, teach theology, write a book, become a missionary. Reasons of health, the long hours . . . ah, how they would cackle with glee in the Curia.

Their cackles turned to beeps, and he was confused for a moment. It was his private phone, of course, although his heart was pounding with the thought that somehow the Curia had been in the room with him, reading his mind. He took the phone out of his pocket and flipped it on. "Collingwood here."

"Hello, Father, this is David Shea. From Fordham?"

"Yes, David, how are you?" And what the devil—

"Fine, fine. I'm very sorry to disturb you, but it's about the conversation we had yesterday?"

"Yes?" Collingwood was suddenly totally alert.

"It may be nothing, but I understand how important this is. You see, one of the cleaning ladies here swears she saw Bernardi."

"Where?"

"At morning Mass. Saint Anthony's Church."

"I know where it is. Is she sure?"

"She's seen his picture in the paper. She didn't know what to do, so she came to me."

"Was he alone?"

"Yes."

"What time is the Mass?"

"Seven-thirty."

"All right, keep her away from there until this clears up if you can, David. And tell her to keep quiet about it. Okay?"

"Sure. What are you going to do?"

Collingwood paused. "I don't know just yet," he replied softly. "Thanks for the information."

"Sure thing."

Collingwood put the phone away and listened to the wind for a while. Saint Anthony. His patron saint. Clement would take that to be a sign from on high. He wasn't totally unmoved himself. But what should he do about it? To act would be to disobey the Pope, to break his vows. Not to act would be to shirk his responsibility to the Church. And he himself would certainly be drowned in the waves of contempt and disapproval that would follow the debacle toward which Clement was blundering.

He meditated for a few minutes, and then decided. If Clement didn't know how to compromise, he did. He would wait for the results of tomorrow's meeting. If Clement achieved nothing he would use the information with a clear conscience, knowing that he, and the Church, had no other choice.

Collingwood suddenly felt much better. He had a handle on things now. Events could be shaped, plans could be made. He rose from the chair and quickly prepared for bed. He would need his wits about him tomorrow.

Clement would have preferred to say Mass alone, unnoticed, but he was the servant of the servants of God, so he obliged the pastor and let most of the parish crowd into the small, cold church. Evidently not everyone despised him, though this was a far cry from the crowd he and his predecessors were used to. He wished he could have thought of something eloquent and memorable for his homily, but he had only a limited amount of eloquence, and that was best saved for Zanla. So he skipped the sermon altogether, and went quickly through the ritual that was far more meaningful than anything he could think of to say.

After Mass he returned to the rectory. Collingwood was in one of the drafty parlors, standing with a man Clement recognized as Claude Bacquier. The Frenchman advanced and kissed Clement's ring diplomatically, but still managed to convey a sense of his opposition and, yes, enmity. "I am here to bring your Holiness to the Numoi's ship whenever you are ready. Zanla was told you would come some time this morning."

Clement hadn't eaten, but he had no wish to. Should he talk to his advisers? Call Fontanelli and let him blather about Curial policy? Give Collingwood one last chance to make his points? No, it wasn't worth it. It was time to act. "I am ready, then. Let's go."

The other two men appeared a little startled. Did they

expect him to be indecisive about everything? "Excellent," Bacquier said after a barely perceptible pause. "I will just alert the security people and so on."

"One item," Clement said. "The interpreter."

"Oh yes, we have one ready."

"We would like Ms.—what's the name, Anthony?"

"Summers," Collingwood replied—a bit glumly, Clement thought. Another one of the old man's headstrong ideas.

"Oh, but that will be impossible," Bacquier said hurriedly. "Ms. Summers has been dismissed from her job."

"Where is she?"

"Well, she is in the compound. We have to keep her there until the Numoi leave, and then she will be handed over to U.S. authorities for prosecution."

"If she is there, then we want her. It's foolish to oppose us on this, isn't it?"

Bacquier shrugged. "Very well. You shall have Ms. Summers. I will go to make the arrangements."

Clement watched Bacquier leave, then sat down and stared at Collingwood. After a moment's silence he spoke. "Will you pray for me, Anthony?"

The question seemed to bother Collingwood. Why? He blinked rapidly behind his rimless glasses. "Of course, Holiness," he replied finally.

"Thank you," Clement murmured, and they were silent until Bacquier returned.

The morning was overcast, and bitter cold. Clement huddled in his seat and looked out the window. In daylight the countryside had an austere beauty that made him homesick for England: a few birch trees alternating with the pines, a distant farmhouse blending into the slate-gray sky, an ancient horse swishing its tail and eyeing the passersby sleepily.

But soon they confronted warning signs and barbed wire and guards with rifles conspicuously displayed. So much for nature. They barely slowed down at the gate, roaring through until they came to a halt in front of a Holiday Inn. Clement wasn't looking at the motel, however. His eyes were fixed on the strange blue craft beyond, which looked to him like some enormous jewel dropped onto the New England landscape.

Or a pyramid—yes, he had heard that comparison as well. Someone had claimed this as evidence that the aliens had helped the ancient Egyptians build their own pyramids as replicas of the craft. But the pyramids were only tombs. What was this then: a jewel or a tomb?

"Ashanti," Collingwood murmured next to him. Clement unwillingly brought his attention back to Earth. The little Secretary-General was standing in the doorway of the motel, waiting for them to get out of the car. Clement thought that he should have expected Ashanti. The UN's ultimate weapon.

Clement emerged from the car and exchanged effusive greetings with the smiling diplomat. Ashanti led him inside, with Bacquier and Collingwood following.

"Perhaps you have time for a short chat before you visit our friends?" Ashanti inquired.

"As you wish," Clement replied, seeing no polite way out of it.

Ashanti bowed his thanks and led him past the front desk into the first empty room—which happened to be the cocktail lounge, bleak and lifeless in the morning light. The decor was Plastic English Pub. In the far corner drums and audio equipment were stacked, awaiting a more appreciative audience. Clement caught sight of himself in the long mirror behind the rows of bottles, and had to smile. "It has been many years since we have been in a pub," he observed.

Ashanti laughed and took two chairs down off a table. "I do not frequent them myself. But special cases require exceptions." He gestured to Clement to sit.

"My meeting this morning is another special case. Does your rule apply to it as well?"

Ashanti laughed again. His teeth were dazzlingly white, and his laughter seemed so sincere it warmed up the room. "I have always enjoyed our visits, your Holiness. Even when we meet under difficult circumstances."

"We have enjoyed them too, although we always seem to end up giving you what you want."

"But I want so little," Ashanti replied, and it was Clement's turn to laugh. Ashanti leaned back in his chair and looked up at the tiled ceiling. "We both have difficult jobs, do we not?"

"It cannot be denied."

"But you know," Ashanti continued, "at a time like this I think I envy you."

"How is that?" Clement asked, puzzled.

"Well, because you have the opportunity to live by your convictions. How few of us have that chance? Certainly not I, nor the President of the United States, nor even the Premier of the Soviet Union."

"We are hardly free from pressure."

"Oh yes, of course, tremendous pressure. But ultimately you are free. If I did some of the things I would like to do, I would be dismissed tomorrow. But no one can dismiss you."

"Don't you think that freedom creates its own burden?"

"Oh, undoubtedly. We all have burdens, though. I am talking about opportunities. A Secretary-General can never become a hero, for example. Oh, he may accomplish one thing or another, arrange a truce here, settle a dispute there. But he must lead a life of compromise. He can never take the courageous but unpopular step. You can."

"Are you seriously suggesting that I can become a hero out of all this?" A slip into the singular there. Had Ashanti noticed?

"Ah, you must take the long perspective, your Holiness. Look at Paul the Sixth. When was it—almost forty years ago he came out against birth control? Many people say that was the start of the Church's decline. But now Paul is being honored by some for that decision. Because what did it accomplish? It set scientists looking for a safer, more natural method of birth control. So now the pill has been abandoned as unsafe and we have infallible methods for determining the exact time of ovulation. The Church is happy, people are happy, and Paul is vindicated. He has maintained the Church's integrity on a basic issue of human conduct, and eventually the world catches up to him."

"You oversimplify the issues," Clement responded uncomfortably. "Besides—"

"Perhaps, perhaps." Ashanti waved away the oversimplification. "Let me give you another example, from my own country. You may remember the cases of Japanese soldiers in the Philippines who never heard the news of the surrender at the end of World War Two. As a result they spent twenty, thirty years in the jungle, because our emperor had told them never to give up, you see, and they would not disobey orders. Had they returned to Japan in 1945 they would have been nothing, just a few more defeated soldiers, to be forgotten in our national shame. But returning in 1975, they became heroes. Their courage may have been misguided, but courage it truly was, and after thirty years we could applaud it."

"Are we then fighting a long-lost war all by ourselves?"

Ashanti smiled and leaned toward Clement. "People do not forget courage, your Holiness. It will take a while— perhaps a long while, if things go badly in the next few days—but eventually your memory will be honored. Why, your Church has canonized men for less, I truly believe."

Clement sighed. The point had been made. "If you could trade places, then, would you do what we are doing?"

"Oh, I do not say that. I am what I am. I do not have your courage. Who does? I would strive as always to find some middle road, to satisfy as many and offend as few as possible. That is all I am capable of doing, I fear."

"Well, thank you for your encouragement anyway. When we are made a saint we will intercede with God to have you released from the purgatory to which all compromisers are assigned."

Ashanti inclined his head in thanks. "You are too kind."

He is not particularly subtle, Clement thought, but he knows it makes no difference. The doubt has been planted. Was this just an empty gesture, an attempt to save his Papacy in the eyes of the future? Was he being courageous just to show that he was still capable of courage?

But did Ashanti think that he had not already considered such questions? Did Ashanti believe him that incapable of self-examination? Perhaps. Perhaps it was the best the man could do at the last moment. It wasn't quite good enough, though. Clement rose and wearily headed out of the lounge, with Ashanti following close behind.

The lobby was crowded, and all eyes were on him. He

instinctively recognized Angela Summers, however, standing meekly behind Bacquier. He walked over to her and held out his hand. "My child," he said, "you have suffered a great deal for your faith."

"I have only done what I had to, your Holiness," she responded, bowing to kiss his ring.

"How many of us have the courage to do that?" he wondered. He gave her his blessing. "Let us go, and see where it will take us all."

The rest of the crowd tried to offer him last-minute information, suggestions, warnings. He ignored them all and walked out into the cold with Angela. The blue ship waited. Never had the burden of his freedom weighed more heavily upon him.

24

Zanla sat and waited, his mind devoid of insights, his spirit afraid.

Tomorrow he was supposed to begin carrying out his threat, but he had no wish to do so. He had hoped the threat alone would be sufficient. If he could believe Bacquier, it did have some effect, but obviously not enough. Only enough to bring the Pope here to talk. There had been too much talk.

And what did he have to say to this creature? He was obviously a fanatic, an emotionalist. He would probably harangue him—possibly try to convert him. Zanla shuddered with disgust. There was much about the Numian *hasali* he found old-fashioned or nonsensical, but it was his *hasali*, his life. Carrying on negotiations with a follower of Chitlan, or someone like Chitlan, would be a true test of his training.

Then what was the point? There was hardly any, Zanla supposed, except that you had to carry through on what you had begun. He could not refuse the only opportunity that had been offered him to meet the enemy face to face. If it was improper to capture him, it was not improper to harangue him in return.

Samish was standing in the doorway. "Pope Clement," he announced.

"Let him enter." Zanla rose and composed himself as best he could. After a moment the Pope appeared.

Looking at him, Zanla felt a sudden, strong sense of displacement, the kind that occurs during an improper bonding, when suddenly you are not sure where you are, or if this you who is bonding is the you who is questioning the bonding.

Why had he expected a young man, full of passion and anger?

What was there about this very different person that made Zanla so nervous, and yet so relieved?

He was old, of course, and dressed differently from the other men Zanla had seen. The trappings of his position, perhaps. But beyond the age and the clothing was something more, something that reached Zanla despite the alien features: goodness, dignity, suffering . . .

And why was that so familiar?

There was no time to reflect on these questions. He bowed and spoke to the interpreter—who, he understood, had started it all. No matter: she was his guest. "I am happy to see you again, Angela. Convey my greetings to your Pope. Does he have a title?"

"Your Holiness."

Holiness. He was not sure he understood holiness. "I welcome his Holiness in the name of the Numoi."

"I am grateful for this opportunity to speak with you," was the reply.

"Please be seated." And now what? What were the magic words that would solve this problem? Did this man possess them? "I have no idea what you have to say to me. I hope that you will tell me that you are returning my crew member. What is the point of saying anything else?"

"I am not sure," the Pope responded. "My experience has been that it increases understanding to meet one's enemy. I will no longer be the faceless monster who has stolen Tenon; you will no longer be the faceless alien who threatens our world with destruction. Perhaps together we can find our way out of our dilemma."

"I do not want to destroy anything," Zanla pointed out. "I only want Tenon back."

"Yes, I understand—and I have no wish to cause you distress. But how can we return him to you, knowing that he faces death for his beliefs?"

This was where Zanla's understanding started to falter. "That does not seem to bother most of your fellow humans," he observed. "Tenon and his sort represent a serious threat to our civilization. We must put such rebels to—

death if we are to survive ourselves. What is he to you, that you want to protect him?"

"He is a child of God," the Pope responded.

This meant nothing to Zanla, and he had no wish to delve into Chitlanian beliefs. So he persisted with his previous point. "You may have different standards for proper conduct among your people. If so, then I respect them. I ask you also to respect the standards of the Numoi. They are not capricious; nor are they evil, in any way that I can comprehend."

The Pope was silent for a moment after he heard Angela's translation, as if there were something *he* did not understand, or as if there were something he wanted to explain that could not be explained. Finally he said, "Tenon will pose no threat to your civilization while he is among us. We simply want to protect him, because he has asked us to."

"*You* perhaps are not interested," Zanla countered. "I do not know. But I know that Bacquier, Aronson, and those like them are interested. And I know they have the power on this planet. I do not know if they would try to conquer us. But I cannot risk my race's survival on their goodwill."

Again the Pope did not reply at first. Angela stared nervously back and forth between them.

"You must face facts," Clement said at last. He spoke slowly and intensely. "Tenon will not be returned. I will not permit it. Perhaps he cannot be hidden indefinitely, but perhaps you cannot stay here indefinitely. In any case, your threat will achieve very little."

Zanla gazed into the man's eyes, and they were steady and unafraid. He felt a surge of anger, and was ready to flout all Laws of Hospitality, to throttle this fellow who threatened his race, who stood between him and vindication. But the anger passed as suddenly as it had come. The truth of the matter was, he had no wish to harm these humans. He didn't even hate this old man who was his enemy. He just wanted to do what was right, and that had become so terribly difficult. His anger gave way to despair. "What do you want from me?" he cried out, forgetting all his diplomacy. "You have put me in an impossible position. If you will not return Tenon then give me another solution.

I am a reasonable creature. Show me the light, and I will follow it."

Hopeless, Zanla thought as Angela translated. The distance is too great; we cannot begin to understand each other. And for the first time since his initial Voyage, Zanla questioned the will of the Ancients. Of what value was any of this? Why cross the Universe, to stare into this old man's eyes and realize you both were doomed?

The Pope shifted in his seat and spoke, very softly. Angela looked at him and said something in return. The Pope spoke again. Angela seemed to become very upset and started to reply, but the Pope silenced her with a gesture and directed her to translate.

"Take me instead," she said softly, in Numian.

Zanla was confused. "You, Angela? What do I need of you?"

She moved her head back and forth in disagreement. "His Holiness says: take him instead of Tenon. A trade." The Pope spoke some more, and she translated quickly. "Perhaps your people will forgive you if you return with one of the most important members of the alien race. They need not know the conditions of the trade. Perhaps they will see it as a bold and daring maneuver on your part. Certainly it could not be seen as weakness. You take a chance that the secret of your travel will be discovered. But believe me, we are a curious, restless race, and simply knowing that the problem can be solved is enough to insure that someday it will be, with or without Tenon. Just by coming here and meeting us you have made it impossible for your civilization ever to be the same again. So you might as well get something in return for that. I cannot tell you precisely how to make bombs or computers or televisions, but I can tell you much—more than anyone cleared by the United Nations, for example, who would tell you only what our governments want you to know. Take me and leave Tenon behind."

Zanla listened closely to the reasoning, but the reasoning meant less to him than a sudden image: of an old man leaning on a stick as he crossed a cobblestoned courtyard, heavy robes draped limply over his slight figure. It was Elial, the last time Zanla had seen him, having forgiven

Zanla and set his course straight for the future, going back inside to prepare for death like a true Numian. All his life Zanla had tried to measure up to the standards Elial had set for him, and always he had fallen short. Just as, perhaps, Numos had always fallen short of Elial's expectations for it. Elial should have been one of the Ancients. He was meant to create, not to carry on.

And here was the source of the image: this old alien, sitting across from him, reminded him of Elial. Proof, if any were still needed, of the ultimate similarity of the races. This man shared the same tired dignity, the same air of having been born in the wrong time and place, the same quiet intelligence. Was this, then, an insight? Should he follow the Pope's advice as he would have followed Elial's?

Another image appeared: Elial questioning. "What is the most difficult action?"

"Tell me, Master."

"It is the one that must give of self. And why is that the most difficult action?"

"Tell me, Master."

Elial put his palms out toward his pupil. "Because we never really know what it is that we give."

Zanla looked across at the old man giving of self. If Zanla accepted, what was it that he would receive?

He did not know.

Ergentil's eyes wandered over the pages of the Chronicle of the Ancients, but for once she could not concentrate on them, they made no sense. Below her, on the third level, Zanla was meeting with the enemy, and perhaps the future of her planet was being decided. Perhaps it had already been decided: it would not be unlike Zanla to tell her nothing, to let her find out from a junior officer that the meeting was over, that all had been settled, that Departure was imminent. . . .

She stifled her anger; it was pointless. What mattered was the result, not how she was treated. If he ignored her and saved Numos, what did she have to complain of? And really, it had not been so bad lately—the shared crisis, if it had not made them as close as bondmates should be, at least had not driven them farther apart.

She sighed and tried again to focus on the Chronicle. She needed wisdom, and this was the only place she knew to find it.

"You set quite a good example, Priestess. I am hesitant to disturb you."

She shut the book and looked up at Zanla standing in the doorway, ill at ease as usual. She said nothing. Eventually he entered and walked past her. His back to her, he examined her austere wall coverings portraying events in the lives of great priestesses. He had seen them a hundred times already. What did he want? "Will the Pope return Tenon?" she asked.

The wall coverings remained quite interesting. She controlled her temper. "Why are you here, if you will not speak to me?" she whispered.

Zanla turned finally. "No, he will not return Tenon," he replied.

She had expected as much. "Then what has happened?"

"He has made an offer." Zanla began to pace. He couldn't go far in the small room. Ergentil's gaze followed him. "He has offered to come with us instead of Tenon. A trade."

Ergentil tried to make sense of this piece of news. "We leave Tenon in their hands, and take their leader instead?"

"Precisely."

"And did you accept this offer?"

His pacing continued. There is no way out, Ergentil thought. The question must still be answered, sooner or later. "It is a reasonable solution to the problem," Zanla said. "At least we get something in exchange for Tenon. The man can tell us much. An alien in person will mean more to the Council than all our notes and reports."

A few days ago she would have screamed invective at him. Now . . . something had changed. She breathed deeply and stood up. Zanla stopped pacing and looked at her. "You cannot do it," she said. "Whatever you decide, Zanla, you cannot bring their leader to Numos."

Zanla closed his eyes. "Why not?"

"Because it is exactly what they want. As soon as this Pope is on Numos he will be in touch with the Chitlanians. His very presence—his very existence—will give them strength. And meanwhile, back here, the humans can still interrogate Tenon. Before very long we will be attacked on two fronts: from space, and on Numos itself."

"Tenon knows nothing," Zanla said. "And we can keep the Pope guarded."

"Tenon knows about the bonding and the *retheo*, which is more than the Earth scientists do. And who is to say that the Pope's guard will not be a secret Chitlanian? Think of the risk, Zanla."

"There is risk in everything we do now. The Pope is an old man. He will not do us harm."

"He can do us nothing but harm. Will he help us eliminate the Chitlanians? Will he help us develop weapons to fight off an invasion from Earth? What will you achieve by bringing him back with us?"

Zanla was silent for a while, his eyes open now, staring at the floor. Ergentil sat back down, waiting for his response. "Perhaps it is time we changed," he murmured, "exposed ourselves to new ideas, looked to the future instead of the past. Perhaps this is where the weight of events is pushing us. Perhaps this is what the Ancients wanted us to do, what they hoped would come of these Voyages: the next step, the next twist of the spiral—"

"It is not your decision," Ergentil interrupted, her voice suddenly harsh. "You cannot risk the safety of Numos based on some muddled interpretation of the Chronicle. You do not have that right. If our future will be as you describe it then it must come without your assistance."

"I am the Master of this Ship," Zanla replied coldly. "The Council has chosen *me* to make these decisions for Numos. Not you, not my officers. I am the one who brought us to these people. I will decide what risks we will take with them."

Ergentil stared up at him, and she realized that nothing could be left unsaid now, no weapon could be left unused. His own words revealed the problem. She would ignore it no longer. "Do you dare endanger our race just to prove you are not a coward?" she asked evenly, watching his body become rigid with tension. "Will you go to any length to atone for your mistake?"

"I don't know—"

"Oh, the Masters are kind, to one of their own. They hush these things up, if they decide you are worthy of a second chance. But of course the Priestesses know: such knowledge is our only power. Arthea described it to me, when she heard you were to be Master of this Voyage. She told me how, on her Voyage, the moment of Departure arrived and the silence was shattered by the scream of a young novice breaking his bond, running in fear from the *retheo*, unable to face the instant when the blackness of the mind can become the blackness of death. 'What are we coming to,' she said to me, 'when such a man can become a Master? How can anything he does be trusted, after such a despicable act?' "

"I am not a coward," Zanla whispered.

"Perhaps not, but you do not think anyone else believes that. And your every action, your every decision must be colored by your need to demonstrate it. You cannot separate the needs of the Numoi from your own needs. You must back down, but you no longer know how."

"I am capable—otherwise the Council would not have made me a Master."

"Look into your soul," Ergentil replied, "and see if that is true."

They glared at each other for a moment, and then the tension seemed to ooze out of Zanla. He sat down next to her on the edge of the bed, his body hunched like a cripple's, his chin quivering. Ergentil thought: what if I were to put my hand on his shoulder, make some gesture to show that, after all, I sympathize with him in his dilemma? Would it help him at all?

Perhaps, but there was still a gap between them. She could not bridge it yet. So she sat and watched him struggle, wondering which of a thousand other arguments she should bring up, wondering if any of them would make a difference.

"I have made no decision," Zanla said when he had regained control of himself. "The Pope is still waiting on the third level. I told him I had to . . . talk it over."

"And now that you have talked it over?" Ergentil asked

softly, wondering why she was not very surprised at this disclosure.

He stretched out his palms. "I do not know."

"If you go, you will need an interpreter," Angela said after a while.

Clement turned to her and smiled. "You are very young, my child. There is no guarantee that we would ever be able to return."

"You should not go alone, Holiness."

He did not reply. He looked tired, and very old. The strain on him must have been unbearable. Angela wanted to hold his hand, to straighten his slightly tilted skullcap, to tell him all would be well. But would it?

The guard began to fidget. Deep in her own thoughts, Angela ignored her at first. And when the guard spoke, she tried to ignore that as well. *It can't be happening again*, she thought. *We can't be returning to the beginning of the pattern.*

"I believe this person is trying to communicate with us," Clement said quietly.

Angela gazed at the guard. She was young, with deep-set eyes and long straight hair. Mildly pretty by Earth standards. And very frightened.

"My name is Sabbata. You are the people holding Tenon, aren't you?"

Angela translated for Clement. "We are not holding him, Sabbata," Clement replied. "He came to us for sanctuary. We have given it to him."

"Yes, yes, I understand. I was his bondmate, you see."

"What is a bondmate?" Clement asked Angela. She had never heard the term before, so she relayed the question to Sabbata.

The alien looked confused. "A bondmate is the one you're together with—the one you reach out to, and your minds become one. Like when you use the *retheo*—when things change, and the power comes, and the Ship—but I have a message for him, you see. If he will hear it. If he is interested."

"We will give him the message, if it is within our power," Clement said.

"Tell him please that I have felt his happiness. Tell him whatever he has done, whatever will happen, I am glad he is happy."

Clement nodded. "He will be told."

Was that all, Angela wondered: no plea for sanctuary too, no new complication, just a simple, affectionate message? It was as if sunlight had suddenly broken through the clouds. It was not the beginning of the pattern but, perhaps, its completion—the closing of the circle. Angela smiled back at Sabbata. Even Clement seemed more at ease. Then there were footsteps in the corridor, the smiles faded, and Zanla returned.

Zanla's face was a blank. He bowed formally and motioned the guard away. Then he sat down and stared at Clement. "You are a very brave man," he said. "I admire you. But I must ask you once again to give up my crew member. That truly seems to me to be the fairest solution to this problem."

"I cannot. I am very sorry, but I must do what I feel is right."

He continued to stare. "So must we all," he murmured finally, then fell silent again. Say it, Angela prayed. Don't prolong his agony. "I am sorry that I cannot accept your proposal. The risks to Numos are too great."

Angela turned to Clement. The blood had gone from his face—she had never seen a man so pale. There was a thin film of sweat on his forehead. "And your threat?" he asked.

Zanla spread his hands mournfully. "I thank you for your offer, but I must have Tenon back."

Clement seemed to be having trouble breathing. "Then there is no more to be said," he whispered. He struggled to rise. Angela rushed to help him. Zanla looked away.

"Your Holiness, should I get someone?" she asked.

"No, no. It will be all right. It will . . . pass."

But in the corridor he had to stop as the tears rolled down his face. "I am too old for this sort of thing. Too old." Angela gave him her handkerchief. He leaned against her as he tried to regain control of himself. "Please don't tell anyone, Angela. It wouldn't do."

Tell anyone about his offer—or his tears? No matter.
She would say nothing about any of it. He squeezed her
hand, finally, and they headed out into the raw New England morning.

25

Clement walked slowly over to the crowd of officials by the motel.

"Can you give us any news, Holiness?" Ashanti asked.

"Nothing is changed."

"The threat is still in force?"

He nodded. "Please excuse me now. I must rest and pray."

"Can't we talk further about this?"

"It would serve no purpose." He motioned to Collingwood and headed for his limousine.

As they drove back to the rectory Clement rested his head against the top of the seat and closed his eyes. He could feel Collingwood's stare on him, but he was not in the mood for explanations.

"I will have to have something for the reporters," Collingwood said finally.

"You may tell them what I told Ashanti."

Collingwood shrugged resentfully. "As you wish."

Back at the rectory, Clement passed through the milling crowds of functionaries, refused luncheon, and went directly to his room. "Keep everyone away from me, Marcello," he instructed his valet, who quickly lowered the shades and turned down the bed.

"Perhaps a pill, Holiness?" Marcello inquired.

Clement waved the suggestion away. He did not need medication, he needed . . . what? To cry some more? To wallow in self-pity? No, no, to rest. Only to rest.

Marcello left him. He lay on the bed and stared at the ceiling, gray with years of soot from a polluted world. In the distance a siren wailed—a fire? someone dying? or a dignitary like himself, being rushed along the highway to

some futile meeting? *Seventeen percent fewer communicants, twenty-four percent fewer baptisms.* The faces
twisted with rage, hating *him*, yelling obscenities at *him*.

He shut his eyes and pressed down on an imaginary ac-
celerator. He had not driven in years. The idea was exhila-
rating: the car immediately responding to his wishes,
faster, faster, until the faces were a blur, a memory, and
there was only himself, in a warm cocoon of invisibility,
traveling farther and farther away: light-years away.

The Apostolic Palace had turned into a blue pyramid.
The crowds were outside, filling up Saint Peter's Square;
none knew the secret but him. *Things change, the power
comes.* Was it he who disappeared, or the crowds? No matter. He was alone, on a new world, and the problems were
not his to solve. The new people were friendly, but they
could not understand a word he said. He walked down a
pathway and raised his hand in automatic blessing of the
passersby, and they ignored him. He knelt to pray, and
there was no one to pray for but himself.

Things change. Collingwood was staring at him disgust-
edly. "It's only a dream, Holiness. Nuns are being murdered in Bangkok." And Fontanelli, the ash on his cigarette impossibly long: "The tax bill, you know, the broken
stained glass." And Capelli, longing to take his place:
"Hand that creature back to whoever owns it." He reached
out to Angela for her handkerchief (*still have it, must return it*). "Too old," he whispered, "too old." She squeezed
his hand, but he still had to walk out into the cold and face
them again. . . .

His eyes blinked open, and saw only darkness. With a
groan he swung himself up out of bed and walked over to
the window. He peered out from behind the drawn shade
at a leaden twilight. Cold seeped in through the badly fit-
ted casement. He returned to the bed, got down on his
knees by its side, and prayed.

Clement dined by himself in his room, and only after he
was finished did he send for Collingwood. "Anthony, I
want you to find out for me how I go about resigning."

"Resigning?" Collingwood repeated.

"Resigning the Papacy. I wish to yield the office as soon as it is feasible."

Collingwood stared at him silently. Clement was childishly pleased for a moment at the effect he had produced. And then he realized what it meant to Collingwood: his own career would be ended too. He would never get another post as influential as the one he had now. His ambition could not be fed on memories.

I am being selfish, he thought. My decision affects too many others.

But that was precisely what he had to escape. Collingwood was not stupid; he would survive. They would all survive. Meanwhile, the man would do his job.

"Do you know anything about the subject offhand?"

"You mean—resigning?"

"Of course."

Clement could see Collingwood force his mind back into its accustomed channels. "I believe a Pope has to resign into the hands of the College of Cardinals, theoretically. A letter of some sort might be sufficient. I should check with Cardinal Fontanelli."

Clement glanced at his watch. "It's early morning in Rome. Don't wake him yet. But work it out tonight—I would like to do it quickly."

"As you wish, Holiness." There was a pause. "May I ask, Holiness . . . ?"

"I suppose."

"Why, then. Why are you resigning?"

"Nuns are being attacked in Bangkok, Anthony. If the Church does not want me then I should not burden her with me."

Collingwood appeared as if he were about to reply, then changed his mind and merely nodded vaguely. "As you wish," he repeated in a murmur. "I will get in touch with Cardinal Fontanelli."

And Clement was alone again, with the deed all but done. He tried reading Newman for a while, but was too restless to concentrate. Finally he wandered downstairs in search of a cup of tea. Marcello was sitting in the large kitchen with a few other members of the retinue. Several half-empty jugs of red wine were scattered over the table. All talk ceased when Clement entered the room, and everyone rose solemnly. He gestured for them to sit. "Enjoy the wine," he said in Italian. "It's as good a way as any to keep warm in this cold land." A couple of people laughed, but no one drank while he and Marcello stood there waiting for the kettle to boil. He was glad when the tea was made, and he could leave them to their simple pleasures.

On the way back to his room he saw, through a half-opened door, the pastor sitting by himself in his office. What was his name? Clement could not recall. He hesitated for a moment, then walked in.

"Excuse me," he murmured, and the priest jumped up, startled. "I just wanted to thank you for the hospitality you have shown us." He noticed the cot plunked down in the middle of the cluttered office. "I fear we have put you to considerable inconvenience."

"No no no," the priest replied hurriedly. "It's an honor, your Holiness. I—you know—it . . ." He stopped, unable to frame the sentence.

Clement nodded. "This whole business has been hard on both of us, I think. I'll make a deal with you: I'll pray for you if you'll pray for me. Then perhaps we'll both feel better."

The priest smiled nervously. "I pray for you anyway, Holiness. But I'll pray even harder."

"Then it's a deal."

He smiled and blessed the priest, who still looked nervous and puzzled. Clement sighed as he mounted the stairs. He stopped and took a sip of his tea at the top. It was going to be a long night.

Collingwood sat and stared out the window—as he had done last night, as it seemed he had been doing so often lately. His phone lay on his lap. How long had it been: two hours? three?

Last night his course had seemed clear. But now, when the time had arrived, and his worst fears had been realized (and then some), it was not so easy. He could call Rome, and wash his hands of the whole business, or he could call the number he had obtained today, and see if a solution were not still possible.

The decision could not be made by thinking about it, he realized finally. Thinking only provided him with reasons for what he really wanted to do. *I have come too far*, he thought. *I really do not want to give up.* He picked up the phone, punched out the number, and waited for a sleepy French voice to answer.

Once Bacquier could be made to understand the nature of Collingwood's information the conversation was swift and direct. No questioning of motives, only the merest probing about sources, then a quick promise of action—and anonymity. Collingwood hung up, satisfied and relieved. Perhaps everything would still work out. He rose and turned to leave the dreary room.

Clement was standing in the doorway, staring at him. "I heard your voice," the Pope said quietly. "I thought you were speaking to Fontanelli." He paused. "I couldn't sleep," he added finally.

"You heard it all, then," Collingwood said.

"Enough."

Collingwood felt weak, almost faint, as he stood there. It was not just the shock of being discovered, like a child with a dirty magazine. There was something unnerving about the way Clement, too, was just standing, staring silently at him. *How dare you?* he wanted Clement to say. *Do I not have enough trouble without having to deal with this act of betrayal?*

But Clement said nothing, and his silence had its own message. No explanations, no excuses. It required something more fundamental, more important, and it was not to be denied.

"Permit me to resign, Holiness," Collingwood said.

Clement slowly shook his head. "Not yet, Anthony."

"The call to Fontanelli? I'll do it right away. I—"

"No, Anthony. I want you to call Bacquier again."

"If you wish. But it can't be undone, Holiness. I'm sure he's already—"

"I understand. I want him to set up another meeting between me and Zanla for tomorrow morning—early, before Tenon can be returned. If they manage to capture him."

Collingwood started to object, but Clement's stare silenced him. "You are not resigning then?"

"I have a job to do. A job you have just made more difficult."

What the stare required was simple obedience, obedience due the Vicar of Christ. Collingwood perceived that Clement had changed, and that he had somehow produced the change. But he couldn't think about that now. He would have time—too much time, he feared—to ruminate on it later. Now he was obliged to obey. With Clement watching, he turned back to his phone and punched out Bacquier's number.

"I am confused, Monsignor. I do not see what purpose would be served. . . . But at such short notice. I cannot understand, particularly if we find Tenon . . . Well of course we are not certain, but . . . Yes of course I will hold." Bacquier drummed his fingers on the nighttable and cursed silently. "Yes, your Holiness, I am here. . . . I understand. . . . Yes, of course . . . I understand . . . certainly, your . . . I will do my best. . . . Yes, I will be back in touch. Good night, your Holiness."

Bacquier hung up, and allowed his curses to become vocal. What in the world was going on over there?

But that didn't really matter. There would be no harm in chasing down one more lead on Tenon; and there would be no harm in setting up one more meeting—except, perhaps, to his own health, going out into the bitter cold night to visit the damn blue ship.

Bacquier stretched and prepared to go to work. Things would be so much easier if West could find the blasted alien.

Zanla sat in his office and tried to ponder the meaning of Bacquier's latest visit. More talk. He was willing to talk, especially after hearing the complaints of the crew when he told them they would actually have to try to carry out the threat. But he didn't see what it would accomplish, unless the Pope changed his position.

He couldn't keep his mind on the threat, or Bacquier, or the Pope, however. It was too late at night, and this was the time when his plans yielded to his memories, the darkness of the outside world entered his thoughts, and he was forced to relive his shame; and with each reliving it grew. . . .

He was sitting in his place as the Master made the setting on the *retheo*, and the fear was raw in his throat. This time it was real, this time the bonds would be transformed, space would dissolve, and when it reformed a thousand things could kill him in an instant, and the odds were good that these thoughts would be his last.

This time the fear of death overcame the fear of disgrace: he broke the bond and stumbled back from the *retheo*, from his crewmates, screaming in fear and self-loathing, now longing paradoxically for a death that would end his humiliation. But the other officers had calmly picked him up and locked him in his room; the bonding proceeded without him, and he had to endure the jump across space without a bondmate, alone amid the ruins of his life.

He had hoped the shame would be private, but what chance, really, had there been of that? Ergentil knew, his officers undoubtedly did too. And his crew? The rest of Numos? The aliens? Did they perhaps sense something about him, some weakness they could exploit?

Nonsense, clearly. But it proved Ergentil's point: he couldn't separate his private problems from his public responsibilities. Just as now he should have been planning a strategy for the final meeting with the Pope, and instead he was staring at the ceiling and remembering events of half a generation ago.

He stood up abruptly and left his office. But in the silent corridor he realized he didn't want to return to his empty room, to dreams that would be as troubled as his memories.

Where else was there to go?

He walked up to the first level and stood outside Ergentil's room. It was foolishness, but he supposed he was past being made to feel embarrassed by her. The worst she could do would be to tell him to go away. He went inside, and slowly raised the light level.

"Ergentil," he said quietly.

She stirred in her bed and looked over at him, shading her eyes from the light. Her tousled hair fell down over her bare shoulders. "What is it?" she murmured sleepily.

He shut the door behind him. "The Pope wants another meeting."

"Why?"

"I don't know."

"Did you agree?"

"I saw no reason not to."

Ergentil looked away for a moment, considering. "Why have you come to me then?" she asked.

"I would like you to be at the meeting."

She could not hide her astonishment, but it quickly passed. "Very well," she said. "I was glad you took my advice during the first meeting."

That was her way of saying she appreciated the offer, he realized. No mention of his initial hesitation, of all his other mistakes. It appeared their truce was complete.

She shifted in her bed, ran a hand through her hair. "Is that all?" she asked—but not unkindly, he thought, not with a tone of dismissal.

"Samish awoke me to speak with Bacquier. I can't get back to sleep."

"What would you have me do?"

He didn't know, he didn't know. "Talk with me."

"What about?"

"About—about the threat. I don't want to have to go through with it. The crew is so tired, the *retheo* settings—I don't know. And once we do it . . ."

"You are the Master. It is your decision."

"I would much rather . . ." His voice trailed off again. And he realized he did not want to talk about the threat, or the meeting, or his shame. Too many words had already been spoken. He gazed at her in the silence; her eyes were puzzled, uncertain, but not—

Of its own accord the bonding started, he could feel her feel his need, he could sense her hesitation, and then the release. She reached out her arms to him, and he crossed the room to where she lay. She enfolded him in her embrace, stroking the back of his head, letting her warmth wash over him like scented oil. *Let it go*, they thought together, *there is only this moment, let all the rest go*, and together they sought the beauty of the moment, and found it in each other.

26

Madeleine West's hand reached out for the phone while she was still asleep. She answered it before the first ring had ended.

"West."

"Hello, this is Claude Bacquier. I'm very sorry to disturb you, but I have some urgent information."

"Yes?" Her husband had stirred at the sound of the phone. His hand came to rest on her thigh. She flicked it away like a mosquito. Her own hand tensed on the receiver.

"Bernardi has been seen at 7:30 Mass at Saint Anthony's Church. That's on Shepherd Street in the Bronx. This information is thirdhand, but comes from a very good source, so it should be checked out carefully."

"Who is the source?"

"I'm afraid I cannot tell you."

"Who did the source get it from?"

"I don't know."

West sighed. "It's better than nothing, I guess." And, after a pause: "Are they going to carry out their threat, do you think? Today's the day."

"I am aware. The Pope is going to meet with Zanla again. That is a good sign. But who knows? If you find Tenon, get him here as soon as possible. If you do not find him . . ."

The sentence trailed off. Bacquier was in the same boat she was in, West realized. His job was to develop friendly relations with the aliens. If this thing blew up, his career might blow up with it. Like her own career, if she couldn't manage to find Tenon with the resources of the United

182

States Government behind her. Damn him. "Give me your personal number. I'll call you if anything happens."

"Very well."

When she hung up she glanced at the clock. Two-fifteen. There would be some mighty grumpy agents in a few minutes. She got out of bed and went downstairs to use the kitchen phone. No sense disturbing her husband.

West slipped into a pew near the back of the church and knelt down. It was 7:20. She was wearing a knitted cap that all but covered her eyes and a shapeless old coat which, she hoped, made her look poor and therefore inconspicuous.

She folded her hands in an attitude of prayer and glanced covertly around her. She wasn't used to churches. This one had an impressive stone exterior, but the inside had been painted a hideous shade of pink, perhaps in a misguided attempt to make it cheerier. Numerous statues gazed disapprovingly out of nooks and crannies at the color—or perhaps at her. They were all bland and lifeless, except for the crucifix, whose sculptor had taken a gruesome delight in depicting Christ's suffering. The thorns in His crown were immense, His face was spattered with blood, His body was twisted in agony. How did people find comfort in religion, she wondered.

She picked up a tattered hymnal and fingered it idly as she watched the old ladies trudge in—kerchiefed Italian women, leaning on canes, carrying shopping bags. There were about a dozen scattered throughout the large church as the Mass began. And not a single man. West felt a stab of anger. Another waste of time. Damn Bernardi. And Bacquier. And the aliens.

She mimicked the old ladies in front of her, standing and sitting on cue while her eyes swept the church. She wished she could talk to the agents posted outside. Maybe Bernardi had sensed something and been scared away. Maybe they were following him at this moment, closing in on him without her. . . .

West heard a noise behind her—the dull thud of a kneeler hitting the floor. She waited. No other sound. She closed her eyes. It took all her self-discipline not to turn around and look.

She was furious—at herself, mostly. If it were Bernardi, then he had the entire length of the Mass to decide that she looked suspicious. Why hadn't she stayed outside? Why had she thought that being in here would somehow help matters? He would slip out of the church, lose the other agents (who were probably asleep), and she wouldn't even realize it until it was too late. And even if he didn't lose them, he was smart enough not to lead them to Tenon.

She tried to calm down. Nothing to be done; just act natural. Why should he suspect that the old lady in the baggy coat was an FBI agent? We are the professionals, she thought, he is the amateur.

Still, she was grateful that the Mass seemed to move so swiftly. No time on weekday mornings for elaborate rituals, evidently. The priest moved about the altar with the brisk efficiency of a housewife setting the dinner table. Before West knew it the old ladies were bustling up to the front to receive communion.

Should she join them? She didn't know Catholic etiquette. It might look odd if she were the only one to remain in her pew. But if she did walk up to the altar it would offer Bernardi (if it was Bernardi) the perfect opportunity to disappear. She waited for a moment in the dim hope that the person would walk past her to receive communion himself. But that would make things too easy, she thought grimly. Finally she slid out of the pew and headed for the altar.

West had never done this before. She felt a little nervous as she stood in the short line in front of the priest. It was probably blasphemy or something, especially if you were doing it while trying to track down a priest. Maybe she would be struck by lightning as she swallowed the host. An occupational hazard.

The priest was a plump middle-aged Italian reeking of cheap after-shave. She realized as she took the host that for the rest of her life she would associate communion with that after-shave. She put the host in her mouth. It tasted like cardboard, and was difficult to swallow, but the lightning never struck. She turned quickly and walked back down the aisle.

She stopped halfway, her eyes probing the shadows. Nobody there. Had she imagined the sound? No, that was silly. Someone had been behind her. And now he was gone. "Bastard," she muttered and broke into a run, as the old ladies turned to watch in shocked disbelief.

West blinked her eyes against the bright sunlight and motioned to Callaghan across the street. She fished her telecom out of her pocket and he did the same. "Was it Bernardi?" she demanded. "Did he get away?"

"Relax, chief," Callaghan replied calmly. "He just turned left onto Dunstable. Dewey's got him. Couldn't have gone more'n a couple hundred yards."

"Does he suspect anything?"

"He looked a bit cautious, but wouldn't you?"

She began to feel pretty foolish. There was nothing to worry about. They had their man. They were doing their job. "Okay, I'll catch up with Dewey. The rest of you spread out but head in our direction. Keep your telecoms on." She hurried down the steps of the church and turned left.

She picked up Bernardi before she spotted Dewey—good for Dewey. Bernardi was slouching along, wearing a blue ski parka with the hood up. Even from behind, though, she knew it was him. At last.

She kept her distance as Bernardi walked past boarded-up brick buildings and snow-covered empty lots strewn with frozen garbage. Not her part of town. Bernardi showed no sign that he knew he was being followed. That meant nothing, though. He would be too smart to give anything away.

He took another left turn and West lost sight of him. Dewey was up ahead on the far side of the street, though, and could still see him. Her telecom crackled to life. "He just went into—looks like a little variety store. Didn't know they still existed. Want me to go after him?"

"Give him a minute." Dewey crossed and turned down the street. She stopped at the corner.

"Just got a newspaper," Dewey whispered. "Continuing down Eliot."

West turned the corner and the procession resumed. Eliot Street was narrow and dark with dingy apartment buildings. She had a feeling that this was where they were headed. "Let me go in first," she whispered to Dewey over the telecom. "When I'm inside, get the exits covered immediately. I'll tell you when to follow me up."

"Yes, ma'am."

There was something in his tone she didn't like. She knew what he was thinking: the boss wants the glory. Well, she had earned it. Someday he would get the glory too, if he was lucky.

Bernardi turned and trudged up a set of steps. West increased her pace slightly. As soon as Bernardi was inside the apartment building she broke into a run and signaled to Dewey, who started giving instructions to the others over his telecom.

She raced across the street and up the steps. Near the top she felt something give way and her knee cracked hard against the concrete. Through the haze of pain her first thought was: it's a trap. Then she looked down and saw the large patch of ice on which she had slipped. Fool. Too eager, too careless. And Dewey was watching her. She staggered to the top of the steps, trying to ignore the pain. Luckily, the front door wasn't locked—she knew she didn't have the composure to jimmy it. She got to the elevator in time to see its indicator stop at three. Another break. She took a deep breath and headed up the stairway.

Each stair brought a stab of pain. Had to be ignored. She wondered if Dewey was pleased. Would they remember to cover the roof? Damn coat was hard to run in. Was this the third floor?

She slipped into the corridor just as a door closed on a blue parka. She limped down to the door and glanced at its number. Then she backed away and got out her telecom. "It's 314," she whispered. "Are the exits covered?"

"Front and back are all set," Dewey replied. "Callaghan's on his way up to the roof now. You want the rest of us to come up?"

Let me give the orders, she thought. "One in the downstairs lobby. The rest up here. Use the stairs."

"Right."

Now, she thought, rest and wait for the reinforcements. But what was the point of that? There was no danger. The sooner she got inside the better. They would think she was showboating, of course. Let them.

She went up to the door. It looked flimsy; a well-placed kick would have done the job, but that wasn't in her repertoire just now. Instead she knocked.

There were footsteps, then a muffled "Yes?"

"It's Mrs. Esposito from upstairs," she said in a strangled, gasping voice. "I dunno what to do, the radiator busted and there's hot water whooshin' all over the place and they cut off my phone 'cause I missed a month. I can't go to the super 'cause they're tryin' ta kick me out anyway so could I use your phone please, I'll pay you, honest."

The door opened a crack. The chain was still in place. Bernardi looked into her eyes, and she looked back, and he trusted her. He let her in.

"Your leg's bleeding," he said to her.

"I know it," she replied, fumbling in her pockets. "Somedays nothin' goes right." She produced her gun and ID. "You're under arrest, Father. Please don't move."

He looked surprised and hurt for a moment, and then just laughed as half a dozen agents appeared breathless in the doorway with guns drawn. "I guess you've got me," he said. "What's the charge, may I ask?"

West shrugged. "Kidnaping will do. Somebody read him his rights. Everyone else fan out and search the place."

The apartment was small, so not much fanning out could be done. West led the way into the bedroom, where someone lay sleeping face down on a messy bed. She snapped up the drawn shade and watched him stir and turn.

He opened his eyes and silently stared at her. She registered his looks: short, dark hair, dark eyes, broad ears . . . and, damn it, she couldn't tell. It was close, but not exact. She knew there were blood tests and so on that would be conclusive, but she didn't have time. So, was she looking at a human or an alien? It was unnerving. "Do you speak English?" she asked, idiotically, and the creature in the bed made no sign he understood.

She broke away from his puzzled gaze, finally, and

shrugged in resignation. He was all she had. "Take him and let's go," she said. "We're in a hurry."

She went back into the other room. Bernardi was standing there, handcuffed, at ease, watched by an agent. "Is that him?" she demanded.

Bernardi laughed. "Tenon? Of course not. It's Pete Rigoli, works in a pizza shop on Eustis Ave."

West sighed. She gave a few orders and limped out into the corridor. Her leg was killing her.

She found out for certain on the helicopter ride to Massachusetts. He laughed—quietly chuckling at one of Bernardi's remarks. It didn't register until she noticed his quick gaze in her direction and then she realized: Tenon doesn't understand English. Not enough to laugh at it, anyway. Therefore this isn't Tenon.

"Bastards," she muttered, and they both grinned.

West looked out the window, not wanting them to get any more enjoyment out of her reaction. Things were bad enough as they stood. Her leg throbbed dully. She hadn't had a chance to have it worked on. And she felt the beginning of a headache. Not enough sleep.

There was also a funny taste in her mouth. She couldn't place it for a while, and then she thought of the smell of cheap cologne and the connection was made. It was the lingering cardboardy aftertaste of the host she had swallowed. Her blasphemy had not been overlooked, she supposed.

It was almost enough to make you believe in God.

27

"We have heard it stated," Clement said softly to the congregation, "that mankind's knowledge has outstripped its religions. The Church fights losing battles against Galileo and Darwin, and people's faith is shaken. Is the Church nothing more than a relic of ancient ignorance, vainly reinterpreting its doctrines in an attempt to reconcile them with modern facts?

"We would suggest that the opposite is true, that science is struggling fitfully toward truths our spiritual nature has always apprehended. And chief among these is the interdependence of all life, all matter. *As you did it to one of the least of these my brethren, you did it to me.* Ask the ecologist, the physicist if that is not a scientific truth as well.

"Always our perspectives are widening, but the moral basis for our response to these perspectives has always been there. *Love thy neighbor as thyself.* Science makes the starving African our neighbor, and the homeless Indian, and the oppressed Cambodian, and we realize our actions affect them, they cannot be ignored. Now we have a new neighbor, and science struggles to understand why, and how. But the moral, the spiritual response to this knowledge already exists, and it is right. If we falter in our application of these spiritual truths, then truly religion's claim to superiority is lost. This is a crucial time for mankind, not the least because these truths are being put to the test.

"That is why we ask for God's blessing on our work, and your prayers. The truths will always be there, but men and women must always seek the strength to put them into practice. That strength can only exist with God's help. Let us stand and profess our faith. *I believe in one God . . .*"

* * *

Collingwood hung back amid the crowd of people out-side the rectory as Clement entered the limousine. Clement motioned to him. "Get in, Anthony."

Collingwood obeyed. The limousine moved off down the highway, surrounded by flashing lights and wailing sirens. Clement stared out the window.

"It was not just self-interest—was it, Anthony?" he said after a while. "You really thought it was right, didn't you?"

"Yes, Holiness."

Clement sighed. "Only God can see into a man's soul. And, I suppose, only He knows what is truly right. There is a diocese open in your native state. Rochester? Albany?"

"Rochester, Holiness."

"I knew you would know. Would you like to be bishop of Rochester, Anthony?"

"I would very much like that."

"Good. Then at least something will have been settled this morning."

Clement stood outside the motel. Technicians rushed by, stringing cables and carrying complicated-looking ma-chines. "What is all this for?" he asked Ashanti.

"For when they depart," Ashanti replied. "Professor Aronson wants to measure everything that can be mea-sured. He believes he can find clues to the way the ship operates."

"Do you think he will discover anything?"

"Ah, science is beyond me, your Holiness. Professor Aronson is a very brilliant man. If there is anything to be found, he will find it. What do you think?"

Clement shrugged. "I am as ignorant as you. I wish him luck."

Angela Summers came up to him and kissed his ring. Then she looked at him with concern. "Holiness, I—"

"Don't worry, child. Everything is fine." He reached into his pocket. "Here is your handkerchief back. It was washed and pressed this morning. We shall not need it to-day."

Angela looked at it, and then silently smiled her thanks.

"Are they ready for us?" Clement asked Bacquier.

"Any time, your Holiness."

As they walked to the ship Clement noticed the soldiers, weapons by their sides, faces expressionless, waiting. Above them, a lone bird circled in the cold blue sky.

The room smelled of sweat, but not the sweat that he was familiar with: its odor was somehow sweeter, riper, more exotic. The walls of the room were covered with posters of men he did not recognize, with hand-lettered slogans in a language he did not understand. The black men sat on wooden stools and stared at him, expressionless. Their weapons lay across their laps; they moved their hands over them constantly, unconsciously, like women stroking kittens.

"What do I want with your life, man?" Kuntasha asked. "That is too easy. It gets me nowhere. Perhaps you think you are brave, but don't you think that, if I could get what I wanted for my people by giving up my own life, I would do so? Any man in this room would do so. But the world is not interested."

"Sometimes it is."

Kuntasha slammed the table with an open palm; the other men's hands stopped moving on their weapons. "You are a fool, man. The world is interested in power. I shoot myself, the world goes about its business. I shoot you, or the Prime Minister, the world takes notice, but nothing happens. I blow up London, the world maybe changes."

"For the better?"

"Maybe. For us, anyway."

"Is it worth living in a world that has been changed in that way?"

Kuntasha looked bored and exasperated by the question, and the archbishop worried that he would grow tired of all the talk. But finally he responded. "Maybe. If the world doesn't change, it sure is not worth living in, I tell you that."

"If you could kill me, and by doing so achieve your goal—realizing I have done you no harm and wish you only peace—would you kill me?"

Kuntasha stared at him for a long while and then stood up. He walked over to the filthy window and gazed down

*at the barricaded street; his long black fingers traced a
meaningless pattern in the accumulated grease and soot.
"Yes," he said wearily. "I would cut your heart out, if I
had to."*

The archbishop closed his eyes. What, after all, had he
expected? And yet, there was the weariness in the man's
voice. It was not the weariness of a man who had answered
too many pointless questions, but a deeper, more lasting
weariness, a weariness of the spirit. The archbishop
thought he understood it. If he did, there was something to
talk about, a common ground. And there had to be a common ground. If there wasn't, his faith was meaningless, and
he refused to believe that.

"Well," he said, "let us put that option aside for the time
being and explore some alternatives."

Kuntasha turned back to him, puzzled, and then erupted
with laughter.

Was it merely a reflection of his own tension, or could
he see the strain in the face of the crew member who
brought him down the tiled corridor to Zanla's office,
could he feel it in that room, even before Zanla arrived,
bringing with him a tall green-robed woman?

"I greet you in the name of the Numoi. This is the Priestess Ergentil, whom I have asked to join us for this final
meeting. She is my trusted adviser."

Priestess. She, then, was the enemy, the one whose religion persecuted Tenon and the other followers of Chitlan.
They stared at each other curiously across the table—*she is
thinking the same thing about me, of course*—and then her
gaze broke away and went to Zanla.

"I have never seen her before," Angela whispered to
Clement.

Curious. Was she the real leader, only now, at the end,
making her presence known? Impossible to say. But the
way she and Zanla looked at each other made it clear that
he would have to convince them both.

"We are willing to listen once again to what you have to
say about our mutual problem," Zanla said. "But once
again it is not clear to me how useful our discussion can be,

if you do not agree to return our crew member. We will not let the secret of the Ship be revealed."

Clement continued to stare at the priestess. Did she hate him, for the threat he posed to her beliefs, her civilization? Perhaps, but he could detect no trace of hatred in her eyes. Was that because he did not know what hatred looked like on an alien face? Perhaps, but even then . . .

No, he realized, she was not the enemy, even if she had murdered a hundred Chitlanians, even if she would personally blow up the Earth—or cut his heart out. She was no more an enemy than Kuntasha had been. Enmity was a false conclusion, derived from the terrifying complexity of life. It was the easy interpretation, and its result was so much suffering that Clement could not bear to think of it. The true conclusion would not end the suffering (which was a necessary part of existence) but at least it did not cause any more—unless one counted a Crucifixion.

Things change, the power comes.

"Zanla, the reason I have come to you today is to tell you that it is too late. The secret has already been revealed."

The aliens were silent as Angela finished her translation. They looked at each other once, quickly, and then Zanla said, "What is the secret then?"

Clement breathed deeply and stared into his eyes. "Bondmates and the *retheo*," he said quietly. "When things change, and the power comes." He paused, then added hurriedly, "We have bonding too. We call it love."

"Tenon," Zanla muttered angrily. "Tenon has—"

"Love?" Ergentil interrupted, speaking for the first time. "Perhaps we are not sufficiently familiar with that word."

Clement paused again, gazing at her now. "It is what you two feel for each other," he said finally. "And it is what I, despite our problems, feel for both of you, for all your race. It is the most powerful feeling of which we are capable, and the best."

"If you think that this is our secret, then why can't you travel the way we do?" Ergentil asked.

"Because we do not yet know how to harness it," Clement replied. "But that knowledge will come. You have heard of and seen the powers of our science. All we need to know is the right question to ask, and we will find the answer. When you leave, the most advanced devices of our science will be recording what happens. The scientists will know what to look for now."

"Your science is capable of much," Zanla said, "but I think perhaps it is not capable of this."

"In that case the mystery will be left to people like me, who know nothing about science, but something of love. In any case, we will learn what there is to learn."

"And once it has been learned, will you use your love to destroy us?" Ergentil asked.

"I cannot speak for all humans, but I know that if I came to your planet through love, I would come in order to love. I would want to bond with you as I bond with my fellow human beings. Others may choose differently, but you no longer have control over the choice."

"How do we know—" Zanla started to say, and stopped. Another silence, an exchange of glances. "We will speak about this privately," he said finally. "Please excuse us."

A dim, naked light bulb illuminated Kuntasha's tired features. The odor of the archbishop's own sweat now mingled with that of the others. "This will not work, you know," Kuntasha said. "The government will not accept it. Or if they do, things may get better for a time, but then the evil will return. The evil always returns."

"Perhaps you are right. But it will not come through us, and that is all we can ask."

Kuntasha shrugged, with the air of a man who would never know victory, only lesser forms of defeat. "I will put the terms to a vote, then." But the decision was already made.

"Is it true?" Angela whispered. "I know what Sabbata said but—did you learn any of it from Tenon?"

"I never said I learned it from Tenon, child. Is it true? I don't know. I would like it to be true, and perhaps my wishes added certainty to my words. Perhaps it is an approximation of the truth, which is all we mortals can hope for, without Divine revelation."

"I hope it's true too."

Clement covered her hand with his.

"Is it true, Zanla?"

"I don't know. How can I know? They are only words. They sound reasonable, but—"

"He knows about bonding and the *retheo*. Is there any way he could have known, except from Tenon?"

"It was a forbidden topic. He did not hear of them from us."

"Then the Pope is right: this is all a waste. There is nothing to do now but return, and prepare."

"Or rely on their love."

"Do you think we can?"

"I don't know."

Ergentil covered his hand with hers.

"We do not think it proper of you not to return Tenon to us," Zanla said, "but you will not be persuaded. Please believe me, we have never had any wish to harm you or your fellow humans; we trust that you feel the same way toward us. We will not, therefore, carry out our threat toward you. We depart instead—with the hope that, if we meet again, we shall meet in peace."

"That is my fervent prayer as well," Clement replied. The two aliens looked defeated, he thought. He felt a rush of pity for them. He did not want to be a cause of their sorrow—but one matter remained. "I know that your people may continue to deal harshly with the followers of Chitlan, and that what has happened here will not change that policy. On Earth it is my experience that such policies usually fail, that people grow stronger in their faith under such adversity. My religion was persecuted once, and now its persecutors are forgotten, their beliefs discarded. Perhaps you are certain of the truth of what you believe, and see no reason to tolerate other beliefs. I beg you to consider how many things there are yet to be learned about the Universe, and the possible existence of truths other than your own. If you destroy the Chitlanians, you end the possibility of discovering their truths. We all have much to learn from each other; please give this learning a chance to take place."

The aliens were silent for a moment, until Ergentil responded. "We do seek truth. That is the purpose of our Voyages."

Did she mean it? If so, could he try their patience a little more? He reached into his pocket and took out the book that he carried with him everywhere. He handed it to Ergentil. "This is a—a testament of what I believe. It is my truth. Perhaps when we meet again—and I feel that we shall—we will be able to talk about such things."

Ergentil took the book and stared at it. Then she reached into her robes and produced one of her own. "Here is my truth," she said softly, giving it to Clement.

He accepted it and solemnly bowed his thanks. They gazed awkwardly at each other for a moment, and then Clement realized there was nothing left to be said. He bowed again to the silent aliens, then walked out of the room.

Angela followed him down the corridor. "You won," she exclaimed.

Clement nodded absently.

"Tenon stays, they go. The threat is over."

"Yes. Over."

They blinked back the sunlight as they stood at the top of the stairs. Then Clement's eyes focused on the scene in front of him: the diplomats, the scientists, the soldiers, the technicians—all eyes on him. While he had been in the ship a helicopter had landed. Had they caught Tenon? No, impossible, God would not be that cruel. He saw his limousine by the motel, waiting, ready to take him outside the compound, to the journalists, the Curia, the bankers, the politicians. The poor, the starving, the homeless, the oppressed, the unloved.

Tenon stays. And Clement stays too. Only for him there would be no sanctuary.

"Not a word, child, not a word," he whispered, and they descended to the ground.

28

The preparations for a Departure had already been made, so there was little to do except carry out the agreeable task of telling the crew about the change of destination. It was the first time Zanla's words had caused them to cheer.

Afterward he donned his ceremonial robes and went to the Room of the Ancients where, he knew, he would find Ergentil.

She stood alone in the center of the room, deep in prayer. He waited silently until she noticed him. "We are ready," he murmured.

"Are you glad to be going home?" she asked.

"I will be glad to rest. Perhaps I can rest at home."

"Perhaps."

Together they walked back down to the lower level, where the crew sat waiting, solemn and reverent now that the moment was at hand.

Zanla went over to the *retheo* and placed the settings in their familiar positions. *Home*, they seemed to say: *that is where we belong.*

"We may begin the Departure," Zanla said.

Ergentil came and faced him next to the *retheo*. They looked at each other for a long moment, and then their minds became one.

The interrogation in the motel room was perfunctory, and got nowhere. Bernardi kept asking for his lawyer, and pleasantly refused to answer any questions. Finally someone rushed into the room and whispered something to the FBI agents. They left immediately, telling Bernardi to stay where he was.

Bernardi obeyed for a few minutes, then decided he was being silly, and wandered down to the lobby. It was empty. He went outside.

The crowd all faced the blue ship. "What's up?" he asked a tall man in an overcoat.

The man gave him a what-planet-did-you-come-from look and muttered, "They're leaving."

"For good?"

"That's what the Pope says."

Leaving, Bernardi thought. Without Tenon. He smiled and stared at the ship, which loomed silent and unmoving before him.

"Father!" a familiar voice cried.

He turned and saw Angela Summers making her way toward him. "The two felons meet again," he said, holding out his hand.

Angela pressed it warmly. "They told me you had been caught but—"

"But that's all they caught, except for a friend of mine who runs a pizza parlor and looks suspiciously like an alien. You've been busy too, I gather. How did Clement manage to get them to leave?"

Angela blushed and looked down. "I've spent all my time since we left the ship trying to avoid answering that question, Father. His Holiness will only say that the Holy Spirit was with him."

"Not a bad companion. Is Clement around for his moment of triumph? I've never seen a Pope in person."

"No, he left right away. He . . . the Pope is not a happy man, you know."

Bernardi sighed. "He's not paid to be happy, Angela. He'll get his reward in Heaven."

"He's still on Earth, though, and that's the problem."

They fell silent and watched the ship again. Bernardi could hear messages crackling back and forth over telecoms. A helicopter—his helicopter?—circled the area and then took up a position off to his left. A gust of wind sprang up out of nowhere. Why hadn't he thought to put on his parka?

"Do you think we'll ever find out the truth?" Angela asked. "About Chitlan, and the rest?"

"I think we'll see the Numoi again, one way or another. But the truth about Chitlan—no matter how much we know, it'll always be a question of faith. Some will believe, some won't."

"Do you believe?"

Bernardi smiled. "I believe it's getting quite cold."

And suddenly Angela placed a hand on his arm and pointed to the ship. It took him a moment to notice. The shimmering was not from the sun, the darkness was not from shadows. The pyramid was disappearing gradually, like a dream dispersing in daylight. The center became dark, and the blackness spread to the glittering exterior, and then the color changed back to blue—but it was the blue of the sky behind it. The ship was gone.

Or perhaps not, Bernardi thought. Perhaps it would never leave entirely; some ghostly residue would remain, if not on the spot, then in the eyes of those who had seen it.

People continued to stare for a long time after there was nothing left to see. "Gone," someone behind him whispered, a trace of sadness in her voice.

"Except for the one they left behind," someone else murmured.

Angela looked at Bernardi. Her hand was still on his arm. "What about the one they left behind, Father?"

Bernardi chuckled. "You have your secret, and I have mine. I'll tell you this, though. I wouldn't be surprised if he ends up happier than either of us manages to be. What are you going to do with yourself now, Angela?"

She shrugged. "I have a translating job to do for his Holiness. Then. . . ." She shrugged again. "What about you?"

He shrugged, and after a moment they both laughed.

"Well, maybe Tenon knows what he's going to do," Angela said. "I wish him luck."

Bernardi nodded his agreement. Together they walked back to the motel and out of the cold.

Epilogue

It was summer. He was on his knees in the hot sun, weeding. He was not uncomfortable, despite his robe; he was used to heat like this.

In the distance he saw the red machine moving through the fields. *Tractor*, he said to himself. Someday, perhaps, he would know enough to be able to help with the *tractor*. There was a great deal to be learned.

He was not stupid, though, and not at all lazy. He would do what was required of him, and more. All he asked was a chance. A chance to—

A shadow moved across his patch of ground. He squinted up at the white-cowled figure looming above him. The figure made some signs with his hands. He nodded his understanding, and the figure went away.

He rose and brushed the dirt off the knees of his robe. Then he walked back to the large stone building at the top of the hill.

Dom Michael watched him enter the small office, and as always tried to keep the curiosity out of his gaze. It had not been easy on that morning when Bernardi had left the poor fellow on his doorstep. But as the months went by and Frater Joseph entered more and more fully into the life of the abbey . . . well, there was less and less to be curious about. Old identities were shed like ragged, useless garments when one entered a place like this; his garment may have been stranger than the rest, but it was evidently no harder to get rid of.

"Frater Joseph, please sit down."

He sat. Dom Michael tried to frame his sentences clearly

and simply. It was hard to know when he was failing to communicate.

"How are your studies coming, Joseph?"

The words came back slowly but accurately. "Very well, Father Abbot."

"I'm glad to hear it. The prior informs me you are making great progress. Everyone is pleased with the way you have fit in here. Now, the reason I called you in from your work is that I have some important news concerning your status." He paused, and made a special effort to be clear. "As you know, you are now what is called an *oblate*: that is, you are a layperson who shares in our work at the abbey but without taking any vows, and therefore without any formal religious obligations. You have asked for permission to enter the novitiate in order to prepare for becoming a full-fledged member of our community. Due to the, uh, unusual circumstances of your case we did not feel we could grant your request without consulting our superiors, so I wrote to our Abbot-General, who in turn took the matter up with the Holy See. The decision came back to us today—surprisingly quickly, as such things go. Your request has been granted. You are now a novice in the Order of the Cistercians of the Strict Observance. Did you follow all of that, Joseph?"

He nodded. "I think so. The answer is yes."

Dom Michael smiled. "The answer is yes," he repeated gently. "You will become a Trappist. The approval came by letter from the Vatican. There is also a personal message for you." He slid a small envelope across the desk. "You may read it when you like."

"Thank you. Thank you, Father Abbot."

Smiling, Frater Joseph rose and bowed. Dom Michael inclined his head in return, and watched him leave.

Our lives are very peaceful, he had told Al Bernardi that cold, foggy morning. *Nothing happens here*. Only in the eyes of the world, of course. The spiritual life has its own excitements, its own intense joys—greater than any the world has to offer. This was one of them.

It would not surprise him if Frater Joseph became quite a good monk.

* * *

"I believe in one holy catholic and apostolic Church . . ."

He would work all the harder. He would pull weeds as they had never been pulled before. He would master the language—the language he would rarely speak. He would memorize the prayers, learn the intricacies of the dogma, become a credit to the Order.

His heart brimmed with gratitude, to all the people who had helped him, but most of all to the God who had led him to this place. Perhaps, he thought, awestruck, it had all been for him: forces stretching across the Universe, patterns working their way out over generations, to enable him to come here and give glory to God. Perhaps Zanla's *retheo* setting had not been random or accidental, but because of *his* presence. *Now* was the time for the two races to meet, so that he could become Frater Joseph, and pull these weeds.

That could hardly be, though. Perhaps it was sinful even to consider it. He would ask his spiritual director. In the meantime, all he could do was to strive to be worthy of such a place in the scheme of things.

"I acknowledge one Baptism for the forgiveness of sins . . ."

He thought of the letter, which had dispelled his last remaining qualms about his new life. If Sabbata was not distressed, then what harm had he done? He could dispense with his previous life with a trace of nostalgia, but without regret. . . .

"I look for the resurrection of the dead, and the life of the world to come. Amen."

. . . because in a sense he had already found the life of the world to come. He had only a vague understanding of Heaven as yet, but he could not believe it would be much different from the world he inhabited now.

When he had finished weeding his patch of the garden he stood up and wiped his brow. A monk passing by in a pickup truck waved to him, and he waved back. He took the envelope out of the pocket of his robe and struggled again to read the final sentences of the brief letter inside.

. . . God bless you, Frater Joseph. You have my prayers—and my envy.

Clement

Envy. When he got back to the abbey, he would have to look up the word *envy.*

From DEL REY, the brightest science-fiction stars in the galaxy...